BAREFOOT CHAOS

BEACH SQUAD SERIES #3

MARIKA RAY

COPYRIGHT

Major thanks to these fabulous ladies:
Proofreading: **Virginia Tesi Carey**
Cover Artist: **Amy Queau, Q Design**

DEDICATION

I dedicate this book to all the women out there who are learning to accept and love themselves as they are. To the women no longer comparing their bodies to other women's. To the women looking for similarities that unite rather than tear down. I'm talking about a group of women who truly believe in themselves as human beings, not just as women. We don't follow a guru...we think for ourselves. We don't impose society's beauty rules on ourselves...we recognize and create our own beauty in whatever form it comes in. We don't punish our bodies with diet and exercise so our bodies become smaller...we strive to live big. We don't contract...we expand.
We don't belittle...we empower.

DESCRIPTION

Chaos - a state of complete disorder and confusion; unpredictable; a gaping void

I spend my days a buttoned up schoolteacher coordinating the senior project for my high school English students and my nights with my book boyfriends, not daring to think I could procure one in real life. It's precise, it's controlled....and boring as hell.

The tide shifts and I find myself with a hippie lifeguard who provokes me as much as he turns me on, a Senior class in upheaval, a crazy Beach Squad that wants to befriend me, a wild twin sister back in my business, and a public challenge to expose my long-held secret for the greater good.

Do I deduce this chaos is all serendipitous, meant to thrust me into my true place in the world? Ultimately, I have to decide if I can kick off my shoes, dig my toes in the sand, and trust in love again.

essa

"I thought you'd be...taller."

I smiled politely, covering my disdain through years of practice. I taught high schoolers, angsty teens sharpening their verbal sparring skills with no filter yet in place. I was used to thinly veiled insults and eye rolls.

And this knucklehead thought I wouldn't understand his "taller" comment.

Amateur.

The least he could have done was wait until we had sustenance before he commented on my looks. There went my chance at a nice dinner this evening. And I'd heard this place had killer calamari.

"I thought you'd be more gallant, yet here we are." I delivered a sugary sweet smile, thoroughly enjoying his confusion. I wondered how soon he'd whip his ancient Droid out of his drab corduroy pants and google 'galant'. I saved him the stealthy phone maneuver under the tablecloth and looked at my watch. "Oh, will you look at the time! I've got to get going. Thank you for the titillating conversation."

Before he could formulate a comeback in that tiny brain of his, I threw my napkin on my empty place-setting and grabbed my bag. I smoothed my hands over my ample hips, tugged my sweater set just so, and nodded my head like the Queen of England.

"Good day, sir."

And that's how my latest first date ended.

Actually, it ended with me in my pajama shorts, blanket wrapped around my shoulders, huddled in front of my tiny backyard fire pit grading papers. I still held out hope that one day, the heat of a man's touch sparking fireworks in my body would end my night, rather than an artificial flame put out by a tank of gas and a scratchy blanket that had seen better days. But it happened to be colder than a brass toilet seat in the Arctic, and I was nothing if not practical, so sandpaper blanket it was.

At thirty-one, I was beginning to lose hope in the hot man department. Thirty hadn't seemed so old, but tack on another year, and I'd transformed into an old maid, if only in my mind. The way I figured it, all the good men would have been taken by now, leaving me to navigate the water of divorcees with emotional baggage and ex's that had to be dealt with. I hated to be a cliché but the ol' biological clock was ticking and I desperately wanted to have children.

I'd become a teacher right out of college, having always known that something revolving around kids was in my future. I loved to watch a developing brain latch onto a concept, twisting and turning it over until they'd mastered it, then storing it in their temporal lobe. I could almost see their dendrites forming and growing, shaping their minds and in turn, shaping our future as a collective.

My personal need for stimulating, intellectual conversation

lent itself to teaching the higher grades. The kindergartners seemed more interested in the placement of glue in unfortunate places. Not my cup of tea, thank you very much. I'd settled into a high school teaching job, focused on English and Literature. The past three years, I was given the golden apple of responsibility for all senior level English classes and more importantly, the senior projects.

Surf City High was known for having a senior project that was actually fun, depending on the day, for all parties involved. The project was called Care Dare, and it required an indecent amount of Care, though that wasn't why it was named as such. The work load fell directly on my shoulders, which was fine by me. If I had to be involved, I'd prefer to be the leader and in control of all aspects.

What's that? Control issues? No, definitely not. I just preferred things the way I liked them.

Currently, I was reading through my next batch of idiotic project proposals by my period four class. Granted, idiotic was a bit harsh, but sometimes I pondered if these kids, about to be set free in the world as card-carrying adults, scribbled out the first things to cross their sleep-deprived minds minutes before their papers were due.

The purpose of Care Dare was to interview a fellow classmate and develop a "Dare" of sorts that would enhance their lives. Most of us needed a solid push to leave the nest and fly. This was a safe environment for our seniors to develop the skill of interviewing (hello, job interviews!), along with spreading their wings and trying things that scared them. They'd be off at college or in the work force the following year and they needed guidance facing their fears and stepping into a braver, more mature version of themselves.

My job was to help them set up their interviews, ask intelligent questions, formulate an appropriate dare, and oversee their final report with conclusions from the program. The biggest headache was making sure these kids took the program with the correct level of thoughtfulness. There was a fine line to keeping one from phoning it in versus making a dare so debilitating that the senior couldn't complete it.

The new stack I was evaluating tonight held dares for anything from ice skating to confronting a deadbeat dad, eating a cockroach to working at hospice. Some of them were appropriate based on the fears and challenges gleaned from the interview process, while others were ridiculous in nature, or worse, so extreme as to be potentially harmful.

When my eyes glazed over, I set the pages aside, turned off the gas fire pit and took everything inside. I locked all the doors, turned off all the lights and went upstairs to my bedroom. I slid into bed, removing my glasses and placing them on my nightstand. The room went blurry and I let my mind wander.

I had this weird, yet delightful, ritual before bed where I'd lay my head down, close my eyes and let my mind travel to whatever struck my fancy. My favorite exercise was to indulge in what my life would look like five years from now. Who I'd be married to; what car I'd drive; where I'd live; how fabulous my clothes would be; what a bright, happy life I'd lead. I'd be asleep before I made it to naming my future children and I'd have a slightly better than average chance of dreaming what I'd been thinking about.

And that was how I woke up the next morning dreaming of hot chocolate. Doesn't everyone envision thick, sweet, rich hot chocolate late at night? You know, the fancy kind that makes you lick your lips and sip slowly so you can extend out the bliss hitting your tongue. Sunday mornings called for a walk down on the beach and today, the best damn hot chocolate in Huntington Beach: Chocolate Dreams.

I threw on a pair of sweatpants, an oversized t-shirt, and some flip-flops. A red Angels hat went over my bedhead and I threw my phone and wallet, plus some pepper spray (you just never knew) into a fanny pack, and I was ready to go.

4

There was a nip in the late October air, but I could tell the sun would be peeking out from behind the fog bank any minute now. I shivered as I walked along the cement strand parallel to the surf line. I should have worn a light sweatshirt, but I figured the lower temps would wake me up and make me appreciate the hot liquid magic (i.e.: hot chocolate) that much more.

When I pulled open the door to Chocolate Dreams, the waft of sugar hit me first, lifting my spirits. What hit me second was the eye candy lining the counter. No less than five male life-guards, in their signature red shorts, stood talking to the blonde owner of the shop, a woman I'd seen on past visits. She was beaming and accepting congratulations from them, for what, it was unclear. I didn't particularly care as I drank in the sight of tan, muscular bodies filling out polo shirts in a way only a thirty-one year old single woman could appreciate.

My nose detected a faint smell of cologne mixing with the chocolate aroma and my body followed, like a dog on a hunt. Not that that was a metaphor I would have normally used, putting myself in the role of dog, but my brain was short-circuiting. I was surrounded by hot men and chocolate, the ultimate fantasy of every woman not concerned with staying a size two.

When I reached the back of the group, I stopped and waited patiently, presumably for my turn to order, but in reality, I just wanted to get close and breathe in their masculinity.

Don't judge.

My recent dates had been limp lettuce compared to this brightly colored smorgasbord before me.

The one directly in front of me was a few inches taller than my five foot eight and he was beautifully dark complected. His thick, black hair was cut short in the back, but long on top, making my fingers itch to run through it and mess it up.

It was as I was staring at his hair, that I heard a female voice break through my thoughts with a loud "Ma'am?" Before I could collect my gaze and reroute it appropriately, all five men swiveled their handsome heads in my direction. My cheeks heated as my eyes darted to the shop owner who had a smile on her face, but was obviously waiting for me to respond to a question I never heard.

When stuck between a rock and a hard place, my motto is 'tell the truth'. And so I did.

"I'm sorry, I didn't catch what you said. I was too busy staring. Would you repeat the question?" I willed myself not to look over at the lifeguards. This was humiliating enough, I didn't need to also see pity or amusement on their striking faces. I heard a few chuckles but maybe that was only because my face was taking on a shade of tomato that didn't look healthy.

The woman laughed and shooed the men away from the counter. When they'd stepped aside, taking all available air with them, she winked at me and spoke quietly. "I know what you mean. I just got engaged to one of them and I'm still pinching myself. I'm Esa, by the way. What's your name, girl?"

"It's Hessa. Lovely to meet you. And my sincere congratulations on the engagement."

"Thanks! I know I've seen you here before, so just a heads-up, these boys come here Wednesday nights like clockwork if you'd like to come on by and stake out a table." She winked at me and then continued on as if the whole humiliating scene didn't faze her. "So, what'll it be today, Hessa?"

"Ah...well, I seem to have developed a craving for dark chocolate, so how about your salted dark chocolate with whip, please?" My face was finally cooling down, so I did the side-eye thing and ascertained where the group of men had moved off to. I'd be headed in the opposite direction.

"Excellent choice. That'll be $3.24." Esa gave me my total but before I could get exact change out of my wallet, a hand reached across me and handed a credit card to her. I followed the arm up to a white polo shirt and then up into the most startling greenish-brownish eyes of the lifeguard who'd been in front of me just a few moments ago.

"I didn't think eyes came in that color." Ah, bullocks, I actually said that out loud.

He shrugged off my awkward comment like the crazy lady I was. "Thought we'd pay you back for making you wait so long to place your order. Sorry about that."

I nodded, but didn't speak, having lost the ability when I heard his melodic voice, which was a blessing for us both. I couldn't place the accent, but I wanted him to keep talking so I could bask in its tones.

His friends hollered their goodbyes to Esa and my new obsession returned my nod and then headed out the door with them.

I followed his exit till I couldn't see him any longer and still I stared out the door. Esa interrupted my befuddlement with my steaming cup of dark chocolate decadence. "Wednesday night. Be here..." She gave me a secret smile and turned away to help the next customer.

I rushed out the door, suddenly eager to get back home and break out my song book. That face, that voice, needed to be written about before it faded from my memory. I wrote songs in my spare time, enamored with the creation process. I played the guitar and piano just well enough to piece together the melodies, but my real love was for the lyrics. It was a closely guarded dream of mine to get one of my songs sold and on the radio. I supposed I'd have to send my songs in somewhere in order to sell one, but I figured one day I'd get bold enough, or drunk enough, to actually do it.

The hot chocolate was as good as I remembered it, and it fed my craving, but it also left me wanting more. I was afraid this craving couldn't be bought, nor would it be satisfied by the new song that poured out of me about a gorgeous lifeguard with the mesmerizing eyes.

I had a new visualization of my future when I laid down in my bed that night.

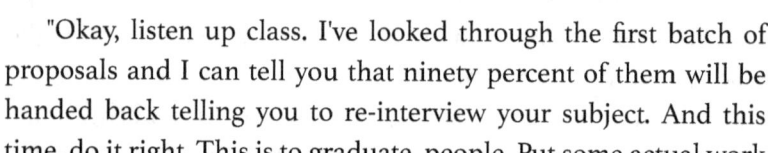

"Okay, listen up class. I've looked through the first batch of proposals and I can tell you that ninety percent of them will be handed back telling you to re-interview your subject. And this time, do it right. This is to graduate, people. Put some actual work into, please?" The bell rang, interrupting my tirade. Just as well. I'm not sure if the students' work ethic gets worse every year or if it was my patience level declining.

Kids rushed to stuff papers in their backpacks and get to their next class before the second bell rang. A new group of kids piled through the door, intent on getting the seats in the last row before they were all claimed. The occasional few eager beavers took the front row seats, all the closer to kiss my ass. I know, that's crass, I really should hold them in higher regard. At least they listened to my lectures and didn't break out their cell phones underneath their desks thinking I couldn't see them.

As they settled in, my eyes snagged on one boy's shirt in the second row. It was lifeguard red with the Jr. Lifeguard emblem on the left breast pocket. My curiosity peaked, I approached him and spoke low so the whole class wouldn't hear.

"Did you do Jr. Lifeguards this year, James?"

"Uh, yeah, I did. I do it every summer." James looked a little nervous, probably wondering where I was going with this line of questioning. I was wondering too.

"Who are your favorite lifeguards?" Maybe if I picked up a few names, I could narrow down who the lifeguards were in Chocolate Dreams the other day.

"Well, we have a quite a few, but my favorites are Kai and Jax." He perked up talking about these guys and I could see the genuine affection.

"You know, we typically have a lot of dares every year that involve the ocean. Do you think Kai or Jax would be interested in working with us?" I was fabricating this line of questioning, but I figured poor James wouldn't question me. Besides, I couldn't seem to stop myself.

"Oh. Yeah, I'm sure they would! They're good guys. You'd have to go through the head guy at the Headquarters building first probably."

"Thanks for the advice. Will do." I meandered back to my desk, wondering if I had the lady balls to take this intel and do something with it. I was guessing no.

"All right, class! Let's talk about Tautology." I addressed the class from the front of the room.

The groans ensued.

"We're gonna talk about Tit-ology??" This came from a particularly industrious fellow in the back row, followed by obnoxious laughter at his own hilarity.

I sighed.

"Patience, Hessa..." I muttered under my breath.

2

ai

"Tower one, I need backup south side of the pier. We got a jumper."

I dropped the radio on the control desk, stripped off my polo and exited the door. I jogged over to the railing, taking a split-second to take a deep breath. Before I wasted time doubting my actions, I jumped off the cement pier, jackknifing my body and dove into the water below. My dive was picture-perfect and I bet I didn't even make a splash as I dove in head-first. My high school diving coach would be so proud.

I surfaced quickly, scanning down into the water for the man I'd seen jump off the pier just moments before. He was flailing with one arm, seeming disoriented, floating a few feet down. I swam over, dove down to grab him and propelled him to the surface. Thankfully he was too out of it to fight me. Once I looped my buoy around him, I swam over to the lifeguard jet ski driven by my buddy Jax. Quicker to get him out of the water on the jet ski than to swim him all the way to land.

We rolled him safely onto the backboard and tied it to the back end of the jet ski. Jax paused, lifting an eyebrow at me and I gave him a thumbs-up in return. Seeing that I was fine after the jump, Jax took off. I took a moment to float on my back, enjoying the sway of the water out past the break. I took deep breaths to let the adrenaline release from my system and let my heart rate slow down.

When I was ready, I swam it back in, body surfing a wave to expend less energy. As I pulled myself out of the water, I thought about how lucky that guy was. He was breathing when I lifted him out of the water and didn't look like he'd broken anything significant. At the end of the pier, the water was one hundred feet below. A jump from there would end in certain death, but he'd jumped much closer in, where the drop was maybe fifty feet. Still a crazy jump, but not certain death.

We got a jumper or two every year, but I saw the guy's face the moment before he leaped. He didn't look depressed or scared. He'd looked excited and determined. Plus, he did it right in front of the lifeguard office window. I'd have to follow up at the hospital later and find out how he was doing.

When I got back to my post on the pier, my supervisor, Ivan, was there to question me about the incident. Ivan was a good supervisor and an even better person. He kept pressuring me to interview for a higher-up position, but my heart just wasn't in it. I didn't want the added stress or the responsibility of supervising other lifeguards. I just wanted to stay where I was, spending time in the ocean where I felt at home.

"What's up, man? You survive that dive okay?" Ivan leaned one hip against the control desk like we were just shootin' the shit, but I knew he was genuinely concerned.

"Wanted to take a little dip and check the water temp. Happened to do that right after a guy jumped in. Lucky coincidence, man." I shrugged like I didn't just make a killer save, the type us lifeguards dig for the adrenal hit.

"Know why he jumped?" Ivan got right to the point. We tried to lock down any word of jumpers getting out because it usually caused copycatters, which required more man power from the lifeguards. And regardless of how effortless I made the dive look, it was risky jumping from that high up.

I shook my head. "Nah, he wasn't talking when I lifted him out, but I'll stop by the hospital after my shift and see if I can ask him a few questions."

"That'd be great. I know the police will do their own questioning, but I want to know what's happening on our beaches. If he's got friends that will try to one-up him out here on the pier, I wanna know about it beforehand." Ivan may have looked chill, but he never messed around when it came to people's safety out on the beach.

"I'll see what I can do."

Ivan got to his feet and walked to the door, hesitated and then turned around. "So. What are you doing on June sixteenth?"

I frowned. "Well, let's see here. Eight months from now, I know I have..." I stopped to chuckle. "I'm just kidding, man. I have no idea what I'm doing on June sixteenth. Why?"

"That's the day Esa and I are getting married and she's hounding me already on some of the details. Would you stand up for me? Be a groomsman?" Ivan looked a little sheepish to be asking me.

"Hell yeah, I will! That would be a great honor. Thank you. Why you embarrassed? It's not like you're asking me out on a date, dude."

Ivan finally laughed. "It just feels weird asking my friends to join in on the wedding formalities. I can't wait to marry Esa, but this wedding stuff seems so silly. I know she's planning all sorts of things and it means a lot to her. I just want to marry her. Who cares about the actual ceremony, you know?"

"Well, hang in there, brother, because your woman wants a beautiful ceremony and I know you can't say no. But I'll be standing up there with you, okay?" I stepped forward and gave him a guy hug, you know, the kind that involved whacking each other's backs. "Who else you got?"

"I only plan on you, Dean, Jax, and Cane, but Esa keeps adding bridesmaids, so I may have to ask a few more guys to keep the numbers even."

"The Beach Squad is growing, huh?" I laughed, remembering how Esa named her group of girlfriends. "Got any hot, single ladies I should know about?"

"Yeah, I believe Shasta is still single." Ivan shot me a smile.

I cringed. "Yeah, she'd be hot if I was ten or twenty years older. But she kinda scares me too, man. I need a woman who's kick-back and will love my VW bus just as much as me."

"You might try fixing it up a bit or even just cleaning it occasionally...that might help draw the ladies in," Ivan added dryly.

"Dude, no way. My ride is a perfectly worn-in, comfortable carriage. The right woman will appreciate her finer points."

"Keep telling yourself that, Kai. I gotta run. Keep me in the loop if you find out anything else about our jumper, huh?"

I hated the smell of hospitals. That smell combination of bleach, potpourri, and death. The fluorescent lights, white walls, hushed voices. I felt claustrophobic in hospitals, and I'd had the good fortune to never need to be in one for any length of time.

The sooner I went in, the sooner I could leave and breath in fresh air again.

The guy's door was propped open, so I stepped in and whisper-yelled, "Knock, knock."

A head popped around the drawn curtain. A man in his late fifties stepped out and asked, "How can I help you?"

"I pulled a guy out of the water today and wanted to check in and see how he was doing. Am I in the right room?"

His face instantly cleared and he held his hand out to me. "Yes, yes. You got the right room. Thanks so much for helping Jackson. He's my son."

I shook his hand. "Just doing my job, sir. Any chance I can chat with him?"

"Sure, come on in." The father moved the curtain aside and stepped back to let me step into the curtained off area.

Jackson, around twenty-five years old, was lying on the bed, sheets and blankets covering him from chest down. One arm was bandaged and in a sling, but that looked to be the extent of his injuries. His eyes were open, but he looked exhausted.

"Hey man, how you doin'?" I stepped up to the bed and lowered my voice.

"I've been better." Jackson started to chuckle but turned it into a frown. "You the lifeguard that saved me?"

"Yeah, I saw you go for a dip and thought I'd join you. They gonna let you out of here soon?" I kept my tone friendly as I'm sure he already got the grilling from police earlier. I wanted him to open up to me and for that, I needed him to not feel threatened.

"I gotta stay overnight. Got a concussion and they want to keep checking in on me."

"What did you to do your arm?" I pointed to his sling.

"Dislocated my shoulder. Doctor said it should heal up fine with rest. And if I don't do any more crazy stunts." He grunted.

"Yeah, that was a little crazy. You do stuff like this often?" I kept my body relaxed but I was on high alert, trying to figure out why he jumped.

"No way, man. But when you get dared to do something, you gotta man-up, you know?" He started messing with his blankets, trying to sit up straighter in the propped up bed.

"Sure, I know what you mean. But I've never had one of my

buddies dare me to do something quite that dangerous. Was it a friend of yours?"

His eyebrows drew together and he looked at the opposite wall. "Look, man. I don't remember. I told the police everything I know, okay?"

Well, that was quick; he was shutting down on me already. I didn't think I'd get anything else out of him. He was protecting somebody, but I doubted he'd ever tell me. "All right, settle down. Take care of yourself. I don't want to see you hangin' off my pier again, you feel me?"

He gave me a quick head nod, which I took as a good sign.

I stepped back through the curtain and outside the room. Jackson's father was sitting in a waiting room chair just down the hall.

I crouched down next to him. "Can I ask you a favor?"

His dad looked all too happy to help me out. "Sure, what's up?"

"Someone dared your son to jump off a pier, a jump that could have killed him. If he ever discloses to you who dared him, will you give me a call?"

He gave me one quick head nod. "I'll give you a call while I'm driving over to the house of whoever dared him. If you get there before I beat the shit out of him, you're welcome to have a chat with him."

"Understood." I shook his hand and left, knowing there wasn't much more I could do.

I drove back down to the beach, parking in the lifeguard lot. I was already dressed for a workout so I locked my truck, put the key in my shorts pocket and took off. I liked to come down to the ocean and go for a run at the end of the day to clear my head. Some days I only went a mile, others I went ten. Just depended on what I had to work through in my head. It was good conditioning for my job, but it was my go-to stress reliever since my high school days.

I'd had an idyllic life growing up in Hawaii where all my father's family was from. I was outdoors all day and even some nights. I was more comfortable in the ocean than I was on dry land. We would fish, snorkel, scuba, swim with sea turtles, surf, stand up paddle, canoe race, and cliff dive. My first language was Hawaiian, though I was also fluent in English. Island life was all I knew, and I had no interest in learning anything else.

That all came to a screeching halt with my parents divorcing when I was in high school. My mom moved back to California, where she had grown up, bringing me with her. I went from tropical beaches to traffic and smog. Running on the beach after school became my way of processing all the anger I felt about the things I couldn't control.

Moana (ocean) was moana, wherever you go. The ocean calmed me so I made sure to incorporate her into my life, even though I now lived on the mainland. Hell, my own name was Kai, meaning the water of the ocean. We were one.

No matter how long I ran, I always ended with meditation. The sun had usually already dipped into the ocean by the time I walked out onto the sand. I'd find a spot near the water's edge and plop down, hands on knees, eyes closed. I'd breathe in the salty air, listen to the waves roll in and recede, feel the wind blow across my skin. Time slowed down and I let my mind wander.

I had a routine. Think about all the things I was thankful for, then shift into all the ways I wanted to live my life, focusing on the feeling, not the material things. Every damn time I would feel my attitude shifting, a sense of calm taking over my body. It was like a hit from a drug, but a hundred times better with only positive side effects.

My lifeguard buddies all thought I was a little weird with my meditating habit, calling me a hippie, but I didn't care. One day, they'd join me and realize what they'd been missing out on. Till then, I'd continue to get my hit of happiness and laugh about how stressed out everybody else seemed to be.

Tonight, I wrapped up my meditation early and headed back to my truck. I didn't want to bother making dinner at my place, so I stopped by Maui Bowl and picked up a salmon poke bowl, extra avocado. You can take the guy out of Hawaii, but you can't take the aloha out of the guy.

As I was heading out the door with my bowl-to-go, a redhead snagged my arm as we passed. I stopped when I looked up and realized it was a girl I'd seen at a friend's housewarming party not too long ago. Jasmine? Jade? Crap, I couldn't remember her name. We'd had a nice chat at the party, but I wasn't interested in anything further so even though she's seemed open to it, I moved on and hoped she got the message.

"Kai? How are you, stranger?" She remembered my name. And she was leaning in for a hug, so I obliged by hugging back, but disengaging quickly.

"I've been good. Just tired after a long day. How about you?" I was taught not to be rude, so I'd carry out a friendly exchange and then get the hell out of there. I'd gotten some red flags the first time I met her that made me feel like she was a clinger and needed to be avoided.

"I've been good, but I'd be better if you'd called me after Ivan's party." She smiled coyly, fishing for a phone call or a date, most likely.

Unfortunately for her, my good manners didn't extend that far. "Hey, I'm all about being up front and honest. I'm not looking for anything right now, so I didn't call. I'm sure you can understand that." I flashed her a smile and turned to leave.

"Your loss, asshole!" she shouted after me.

I didn't even bother looking back. Dodged a bullet with that one. Glad to know my instincts were still in working order.

As I let myself into my one-bedroom apartment, I glanced

around at the mostly empty rooms. Contrary to what I told psycho-girl, I was indeed looking for a relationship. I was thirty-two years old. I wanted to have a partnership with someone who got me. I wanted to have kids and a house full of laughter and warmth. But I'd seen the devastation from my parents' divorce, and I didn't want that for me. I wasn't going to settle. I would wait. I would find a woman who wanted me, in sickness and health, rich or poor. She'd understand my need to be outdoors, she'd want to travel to various islands with me, she'd meditate with me in the sand and enjoy the simple life. And she had to like my VW...deal breaker right there.

She was out there. I could feel it.

So tomorrow, I'd meditate again and I'd send out my request to the universe. It was time. I was ready.

essa

Our entire student body was crammed into the main gym's bleachers. Today was Career Day and we had several speakers lined up to present and then the senior class would go around from booth to booth talking to professionals about potential career options. As you could imagine, it was total chaos, each kid trying to talk over the others, meaning everyone was shouting and no one was listening.

I settled back into my chair on the gym floor, my thick reading glasses in place. Teachers sat on either side of me waiting for our Principal to start the presentation. I had a notebook out on my lap and a fresh pen. You never knew when inspiration would strike and since I was the one coordinating all the Care Dares, I kept my mind open for dare ideas that might help my students.

I kept shifting on my chair, trying to find a comfortable spot. After last weekend's run-in with the pack of lifeguards, I went a bit crazy. I'd met them looking my grungiest, and when I looked through my wardrobe, I realized I didn't have much of anything that seemed sexy or racy or even halfway interesting. How could I possibly show up to a Wednesday night Chocolate Dreams hangout of hotties when I had nothing but schoolmarm clothes to wear!

That observation obviously led to thoughts of undergarments. And my granny panties. Which led to a quick trip to Fashion Island to get my hands on some lacy thongs. Which I was wearing right now and quickly realizing was a big mistake.

The lace was scratchy, rubbing against some delicate areas that had never experienced sandpaper, I mean, lace. And there just wasn't enough material to keep it from flying right up the crevice like a slick piece of floss cutting into your gums. Except, you know, in my unmentionables. The more I shifted, the higher they went.

Was it possible to chafe from thongs so badly you bled?

I was cut off from this terrifying train of thought by our Principal finally taking to the microphone.

"Settle down now." He raised his hand and gave the look of death to our student body, signally he meant business. The kids quieted down and gave a good show of listening.

"As you know, today is Career Day here at Surf City High. For our seniors, this is especially important as we prepare you to head off into the real world and hold down jobs to support yourselves. I expect all of you to listen with respect to our presenters here today. They are here, donating their own time, to talk to you about potential career paths that may be open to you. Without further ado, please join me in welcoming Kai Kāne from the Huntington Beach Lifeguards."

There was a louder than normal smattering of applause, probably because this was one of the lifeguards that worked with the Jr. Lifeguards over the summer, like my student James had said. I looked over at the man approaching the microphone and promptly dropped my pen on the wood floor, along with my stomach.

I was gobsmacked.

That was my lifeguard. The one who bought me hot chocolate. The one that made my insides feel like they were on fire. The one who prompted the ill-fated underwear purchase.

His attention was on the students as he began his speech, so I did what any hot-blooded woman would do. I pushed my glasses back up my nose and raked my gaze over his body, taking the time to memorize the look of his hands, the muscles in his forearms, and the tattoo on the back of his calf.

He looked strong. He looked interesting. He looked hot.

My face was heating up again and I willed it to behave. I couldn't even tell you what he was saying. I was just listening to the sound of his voice wafting over me as I sat stock still taking in all his finer details. I wasn't one to wax eloquent over a man's physique, but it was like my hormones decided to riot the minute I laid eyes on him.

Kai.

I had a name now. I gulped when I thought about what I could do with that information. Probably nothing, but I didn't see my obsession with this man just going away on its own. Twice now he'd stolen my breath and pumped blood into my cheeks from somewhere else in my body where it was most likely needed more. I was having heart arrhythmia and he was responsible.

Loud clapping broke me out of my medically unstable trance. Kai was smiling at the kids and then he was walking away to sit back down with the other presenters. I even liked his walk. It was manly yet sensual, if that even makes sense. It was like he was so comfortable with his body, he could have been walking down at the beach by himself or like now, in front of hundreds of students. It wouldn't have mattered.

Damn, confidence was sexy as hell.

The other presenters kept coming and I managed to take

some paltry notes. My attention was shot and all I could think about was how to make my move. Desperate times called for desperate measures, you know?

The assembly finally ended, but I planned to stick around and make sure my seniors were striking up conversations with the professionals in the booths lining the walls of the gym. In the mass of bodies exiting the gym, I lost track of Kai's location.

"Ms. Woodland?"

A student materialized next to me, looking up tentatively.

"Yes, Grace?"

"Can you go with me over to the booth over there? There's a female entrepreneur that I want to talk to. But I'm kinda nervous." She was wringing her hands and I felt bad for her. Of course, I'd help, that was my job. Never mind that I was letting my future husband walk out of the gymnasium before I'd had a chance to approach and make things awkward.

"Sure, kiddo, let's go." I marched her over to where she pointed, seeing a woman standing behind the table with a few students clustered around.

As we got closer, I realized it was Esa, the lady who owned Chocolate Dreams.

It was like the universe was sending me bright neon pink signs, that looked a lot like Cupid's arrows, pointing me to my lifeguard. I refused to believe in coincidence.

Esa caught sight of me and she broke out into a big, friendly smile. "Hessa, right?"

"Yes! Great memory." I smiled back at her. "One of my students, Grace, would like to meet you and talk to you about starting your own business." I gently pushed Grace up closer to Esa, who reached over the table and grabbed Grace's hand in a hearty hand shake.

"Hi Grace! Come here, Hessa, join me." Esa pulled me around the table and put me right next to her, her arm around my waist.

All my friends from college had moved away over the years,

and I hadn't made a whole lot of new ones here in HB. I wasn't used to all the touching and had forgotten what it felt like to be instantly accepted.

It felt nice.

Esa asked all kinds of questions to the group of girls hanging out at her booth. She encouraged them, gave them sound advice and told them to come see her at her shop. The hot chocolate would be on her. I couldn't have asked for a kinder role model for my female students.

When the girls reluctantly moved on to another booth, Esa dropped her arm and moved us further back in the booth for some privacy.

"So what happened?" She looked at me like I knew what she was talking about.

"Come again?"

"Where were you last night? You know? Wednesday night? Chocolate Dreams? Lifeguards?" She rolled her eyes at me, but softened it with a smile.

"Oh. Well, I'm planning on swinging by one of these days, but to be honest, I didn't feel my wardrobe was up to snuff."

She burst out laughing, laying her hand on my arm. "Oh, Hessa. I like you."

"Thank you, I like you too," I answered truthfully.

That got her laughing harder. She collected herself finally and whipped out her phone. "What's your number?"

"My number?"

"Yes. What's your phone number, girlie? We're going to make plans to get together. My bestie, Bailey, is a personal shopper. We'll help you get your clothes 'up to snuff.'" She giggled at that and waved her phone at me.

It felt kind of like I was a charity case but desperate times, remember? I gave her my number and we planned to meet up Sunday morning.

A new group of kids crammed into her booth, so I left her to charm their socks off while I perused the other booths. I was just walking from her booth to the next, not looking where I was going as I was discombobulated by my new friend, when I ran into a warm body. Hands grabbed my arms and steadied me before I could ricochet off and hurt myself. Which was fortunate because walking in these heels on a slick, wood floor was hard enough without being a human pinball.

"My apologies." The velvety voice sang to me.

A shiver ran down my spine and my thong chafing turned surprisingly sexual in nature. It could only be one man.

"Kai," I muttered, eyes wide in surprise.

He cocked his head and those hazel eyes turned green as they swept me from head to toe and back up again. "Do we know each other?"

Well that was just awkward. I'd called him by name, like the fantasizing crazy woman I was, when we'd never actually met. "I-I saw your speech earlier. Kai Kāne, right? Is that Hawaiian?"

There. That was normal. I was about to pull myself upright, my dignity restored, when I realized his hands were still on my arms, holding me in place. I liked those hands on my arms. Maybe I should try tripping and bumping into people more often if it had this effect.

He flashed his straight, white teeth at me, those eyes never leaving my face. "Yes, it's Hawaiian. How'd you know?"

"I'm an English teacher. Sort of a nerd for words and language. I find Hawaiian to be particularly beautiful with all the vowel usage."

"Ah, I see. Do you have a name too, teacher?" He smirked at me, his hands trailing off my arms, causing goose bumps to appear.

"I do, though not as alliterative as yours, I'm afraid." I used my newly freed arms to push my glasses up and take a step back. The oxygen level that close to him was lower than normal air or something. I couldn't seem to catch my breath.

He chuckled, causing the cutest dimple to appear on his cheek. How did one man get all the good genes? Statistically, he had to have some of the negative ones too. Maybe he'd go bald early or develop halitosis.

"My mother had a thing for alliteration, but I'd much prefer to know your name, alliteration or not." He was still throwing the dimple out there, which is why my brain short-circuited and I didn't tell him my name earlier. It was a powerful weapon, he should use it sparingly.

"Oh! Right. Sorry. Yes, I'm Hessa Woodland." I stuck my hand out.

He grabbed hold of my hand, but didn't shake it. Just held it.

It was awkward. It was warm. It was nice. It should never end.

"Nice to officially meet you, Hessa."

"Ms. Woodland, are you coming?" I whipped my head to the side and saw Grace standing there, waiting for me it seemed. I looked around and most of the kids had exited the gym, off to their next class.

I jerked my hand out of Kai's grasp, coming back to reality and realizing I couldn't be standing around holding hands with a man in front of the whole school. I didn't want a resurgence of my grade-school nickname from a particular nasty bully: Hessa the Hussy. I didn't mind being a hussy, but behind closed doors. A girl had to have boundaries.

"Nice to meet you too, Kai. See you around." I couldn't look him in the eye, instead, hustling around him to catch up to Grace and get to my classroom on time. The thong was back to straight chafing, the sexy leaving my body the further I got away from Kai.

"I hope I'll see you around..." I'm pretty sure that's what he said as I walked off, but I wasn't about to turn around and confirm.

Kai

I watched her walk away, her hips swaying in that dress of hers, the heels bringing up desires that weren't appropriate for school grounds. I'd never had a librarian fetish before, but I was starting to see the appeal. The long, blonde hair pulled back in a demure ponytail, the black-rimmed glasses, the prim and proper sweater over a tight pencil skirt.

And her skin. She was pale and soft and warm. I'd wanted to have my hands on her as long as I could, enjoying the blush that spread over her face just from a simple touch.

Where did this woman come from and how could I see her again? That was my only thought as I stared at the door through which she'd left me.

"Yo, earth to Kai."

I spun around and found Esa smiling at me, arms crossed over her chest.

"What's up, Esa?" I wasn't sure how much of that she'd seen.

"What the hell was that?" Her smile turned slightly evil.

Okay, clearly she'd seen a lot. "I'm not sure what that was, but I do know I'm gonna track down Ms. Woodland." No sense pretending otherwise. When my intuition said to go for something, I knew better than to ignore it. And right now? My intuition was screaming Hessa's name.

"Not that I know anything, but just make sure you come to Chocolate Dreams on Wednesday. I have a feeling she might be there..." Esa raised an eyebrow before spinning around and walking back to her booth and packing up her table.

Looks like I had plans Wednesday night.

Hessa

I walked into Nordstrom, my purse shaking in its boots. You know, if it had feet. My wallet had never been taken out of my purse in Nordstrom before and she could feel the highly priced charge in the air. Before I could question my decision, Esa waved her arms in the air across the aisle by some dresses that looked more appropriate for prom.

I made my way over, seeing another woman by her side. A really beautiful woman. With the trendiest outfit clinging to her every curve. Hair, make-up, and accessories so on point I wondered if she stepped right out of a fashion magazine. The butterflies in my stomach took flight, and I felt completely out of place in my khakis and plain shirt.

"Hessa! I'm so glad you're here! Hessa, this is Bailey. Bailey, meet Hessa." Esa put her arm around me again and waived her other hand to Ms. Gorgeous.

Bailey smiled warmly. "Nice to meet you, Hessa. I've heard great things about you! I can't wait to come up with outfits for you today. Are you looking for things for work or personal life?" She linked arms with me and pulled me out of the dress section, waiting for my answer.

"Um, I think a little of both. A few work pieces, but mostly I need casual wear and maybe a few date night outfits." My stomach was settling just being around Bailey. She may be gorgeous and intimidating, but she was equally friendly.

"All righty. Let's get the casual wear stuff first and then once we're warmed up we'll get the date night outfits. Sound good?"

I nodded my acceptance. From there, it was a whirlwind of Bailey grabbing hangers and then I found myself in a huge dressing room. I was embarrassed to change in front of Bailey, but she just buzzed around getting things off hangers and arranging the clothes on me, which took all the humiliation out of it.

We decided on three pairs of jeans (ripped jeans are in style, who would have thought I'd pay for brand new jeans with rips already in them), four shirts, one fake leather jacket that makes me look like a straight badass, and two pairs of ankle boots. Bailey threw in a few bras and a pile of underwear.

"Oh, I don't know. I don't find thongs very comfortable." I just can't see paying more money for those torture devices.

Bailey tilted her head, a knowing smile on her face. "Where did you purchase the thongs?"

"Target?" Yes, I said it as a question, knowing the answer wouldn't be the right one based on Bailey's calculating gaze.

"Come here, Hessa." Bailey stood there with thongs overflowing her two hands. "Grab a handful, would you?"

Well now, this was getting awkward again. We were all alone in the fitting room, caressing lacy underwear. My girlfriends in college were the studious-nose-in-a-book kind, not the feel-up-underwear-and-talk-about-sex kind.

Although, the thongs I held now did seem to have a different feel to them.

"Do you feel that material? Without looking at it, can you even detect a seam?" I was about to answer her, but decided correctly the question was rhetorical. Bailey looked dead serious and was on a roll. "No, you can't. Why? Because that's quality right there. You get what you pay for, and I believe your lady parts deserve the very best. Don't you?"

I swallowed, hoping she was done. "I think I'll get some thongs."

She nodded at me and I felt palpable relief, knowing I'd finally landed on a correct answer.

"How's it going in there?" Esa's voice came through the fitting room door, breaking the tension. "I've got coffee."

"Bless you, my friend." I swung the door open and snagged a cup out of her hands before letting her step into the room.

"Perfect timing. I'll go find some date night outfits while you two take a break." Bailey grabbed the other cup out of Esa's hand and swept out of the room.

"Hey! That one was mine..." Esa pouted for all of three seconds before she swung her gaze to me, brightening to a grin. "So. Date night outfits. Got any dates lined up? Let's talk about it."

Between the two of them, I felt like I'd stepped into an alternate universe where conversation boundaries didn't exist and energy levels never dipped.

"No. No dates lined up right now. But I'd like there to be." It was humbling to admit. Here was Esa, younger than me by a couple years, and she was engaged.

"I have a feeling that's going to change for you soon, Hessa-dear." She winked at me and lowered her voice. "I saw you have a 'moment' with Kai the other day at Career Day."

The statement hung in the air and I didn't know how to respond. Did we have a 'moment'? Was she friends with Kai because of her fiancé? And if so, did I dare tell her how I felt about him?

I was saved from answering by Bailey entering the room loaded down with more clothes.

"Okay, I pulled an LBD, which every woman should have, a few more casual dinner outfits, and just a few colorful things for fun." She hung it all up on the hooks on the wall, then spun around to look at us. "Why is it so silent in here?"

"I was just questioning Hessa here on her dating prospects. She and Kai had an interesting exchange the other day and I wanted to know what was going on," Esa spilled.

"Reaaallllyyyy?" Bailey's eyebrows went up in her hairline.

"I don't know if I'd call it a 'moment' but he's a very nice man to look at," I admitted.

"Very nice? That's like how you'd describe the eighty-year-old next-door neighbor or that tomato soup at that place off Magnolia. Give us something better, girlie." Bailey folded her arms over her chest and gave me an encouraging smile.

I blew out a big breath, boosted by the caffeine, and launched into it. I told them how I felt when I first saw him, how he bought me a hot chocolate, and the conversation in the gymnasium. When I finished they both had smiles on their faces and looked ready to jump up and down in excitement.

Bailey clapped her hands and whipped the LBD off the hanger. "We better get back to work so you have something to wear when that boy asks you out. Mark my words: he'll ask you out. I've gotten to know the habits of these lifeguards. It's just a matter of time."

I walked out of the store with my bank account several paychecks lighter, but my heart lighter too. I'd found friends and I'd found courage and hope. Which was priceless, really.

4

ai

It'd only been two days, but I was finding it hard to focus on my job when all I could think about was that teacher walking away from me, the way she'd looked at me, the way I'd felt around her. It was ridiculous, really. She was completely not my type. I wanted a woman who was low maintenance, not a prim and proper teacher in heels and a sexy skirt. One who could hang with me at the beach all day, not fry the moment her skin was touched by the sun. A woman content to get her hands dirty in nature, not study the nuances of various languages from the safety of a book or computer.

Yet. I couldn't get her out of my mind. So I took the leap of logic most besotted fools do and decided I needed to see her again. See her faults, be annoyed by her quirks. That would cure me. In the meantime, I'd keep reminding myself to focus on my job and let the rest go. Time to rely on my meditation skills that were supposed to have trained my brain to focus.

Mid-shift on Monday, I was glad for the concentration because I spotted a guy carting a shortboard out into the water north of the pier, directly in front of my tower. He didn't have a wet suit on which was my first clue he wasn't an experienced surfer. That and he never stopped to watch the sets come in. He just walked right into the water and plopped down on his board. He paddled out by the pier which was normal, but instinct told me to keep my eye on him.

After he'd made it out past the break, he straddled his board and it was so short, only the very tip of it was still out of the water as he waited for a wave. He didn't wait long. Laying flat on the board, he started frantically paddling, trying to catch a wave that he wasn't fast enough for. He attempted to stand and the wave crashed over his head. I lost sight of him as he went under in the white water, taking a hard hit.

I grabbed the phone and called it in, grabbed my red buoy and raced down the sand. I did the high knees run once I hit the water in a run-and-swim entry. I hadn't seen him surface and his board shot by me, on its way to shore. I swam out where I last spotted him. I dove down and spotted him floating approximately three feet below the surface. I pulled him up, laying him on my buoy and towed him in. By the time I reached the shore, a lifeguard truck from headquarters had pulled up. Ivan and Jax jumped out to start assessing the victim as I tried to catch my breath and fill them in on what happened.

They'd just started chest compressions when he coughed and spit out some ocean water. Knowing he'd make it, I collected his board from the sand where it washed up and brought it up to the truck. Once he was stable, we loaded him up in the truck and they took off.

I grabbed my buoy and headed back to my tower. Crossing the sand, I heard a group of people talking about the guy I just rescued. Something they said caught my attention, prompting me to approach them.

"Sorry to interrupt. Did you say something about a dare?" That was the exact word Jackson had used in the hospital.

One of the guys spoke up. "Yeah, when they got him sitting up, he was saying that he'd just been trying to 'do his dare'." He used his hands to make air quotes.

I could feel a frown taking over my face at this news. "Did he say anything else?"

"No, man. That was it. I thought maybe he was doing the Care Dare that Surf City High does, but he looked too old to still be in high school."

I grunted and thanked him for his help. I continued up the sand to my tower, waving off the replacement lifeguard, letting him know I was ready to hold my position again. All afternoon I tossed the words around in my head. Could my last two saves be about this Care Dare thing? Was it coincidence? Sounded like I'd be paying a visit to Hessa's school again soon.

Wednesday rolled around and I found myself rushing to finish my shift so I'd have time to shower before I headed to the high school and then to Chocolate Dreams for our weekly meet-up. I told myself I was just washing off the salt water, but I was spending a ridiculous amount of time getting my hair to lay flat with some new gel I just bought. Disgusted with myself, I washed my hands and grabbed my keys, forcing my current hair to be good enough.

I probably wouldn't even see Hessa.

I entered the school office ten minutes before classes got out. I asked for the teacher coordinating the Care Dare program while flashing my lifeguard information and was told to head to room 207. I'd done some research the last two days and learned what the program was all about. It sounded ridiculously dangerous and unnecessary. Challenging hormonal teens to do things they were scared to do? What purpose did that serve except to give me job security rescuing them?

A loud bell rang and all the doors on the second floor flung open, spitting out hordes of kids as they rushed to get off campus as quickly as possible. I waited until the door to room 207 closed again and no further students exited. I thought I should knock, but then thought better of it. Who knocks politely at a high school?

I whipped the door open, ready to reason with the teacher behind this asinine program. What I actually did was take a step into the classroom and drop my jaw on the floor.

Bent over, hands in a bottom drawer of the desk at the front of the room, was the most delectable ass I'd ever seen. A grey skirt was pulled tight over a round bottom, hips my hands itched to hold onto, and a pair of legs on display from the skirt's slit up the back. Black stilettos topped off the porn-star pose. All thoughts of why I was here drained from my head, leaving me horny and confused.

Then the person attached to said ass, straightened up and spun around, hearing my audible gulp.

"Heavens to Betsy! Wha-- What are you doing here?" Hessa's voice came out breathless, from between plump lips defined by red lipstick. Her hand lay over her chest, highlighting the rapid rise and fall of her breasts from behind yet another sweater set, this time in royal blue.

Her glasses were sliding down her nose again and I took a step forward to push them up for her. She straightened up, pushing her shoulders back. Her movement stopped mine in my tracks.

That's right. I wasn't here to touch her. Or oggle her delicious body. I was here about Care Dare.

I took a deep breath, elongating the exhale, hoping to clear my dangerous thoughts and stay focused on the task at hand. When I felt like I was at least partly under control, I took the final steps to put me in front of her, a safe distance kept between us.

"I'm sorry to have startled you, Hessa. I'm here to speak to the teacher in charge of the senior Care Dare program." There. That came out perfectly calm.

"You're speaking to her." Hessa spun around her desk and had a seat in her chair, crossing one leg over the other, causing her skirt to climb a few inches shorter. Did she wear these clothes in front of hormonal teenagers?

She motioned for me to have a seat in the first student desk before her. I sat, though I preferred to stay standing where I could see her legs from behind the desk. The deciding factor was the uncomfortable tightness of my shorts. I didn't need her to see that if this conversation were to stay strictly business.

"What is it you want to know?" she asked when I was seated.

"Could you tell me about the program? Why the dares? What kind of dares? Who oversees the dares?" I kept my tone friendly. I'd learned early on to remain calm. Getting angry only put the other person on guard and kept you from seeing eye-to-eye.

She tilted her head and looked down her nose at me, making me wonder if that was the face her students saw on a daily basis. "I'd be happy to answer your questions if you would first tell me why the sudden interest in my program."

I studied her face, trying to decide if I should tell her what was happening on my beach, or remain vague and hope she still talked to me. What I saw of her at Career Day convinced me to be straight with her. She genuinely cared for her students, I'd bet my life on it.

I leaned forward, resting my forearms on the small piece of wood that was supposed to be a desk surface attached to my metal chair. "I've pulled two people out of the ocean in the last week. Both of them referenced a 'dare' that made them do stupid stunts. I want to know if these incidences could have anything to do with your Care Dare program."

Her eyes widened as I spoke. "Absolutely not, Kai." She leaned forward on her desk too, close enough now I could drown in her golden brown eyes. Eyes that looked like they'd lived lifetimes already and were five steps ahead of me. "As you may have noticed, it's called a Care Dare. Meaning lots of time, supervision, and *care* go into these dares. *Never* do we allow a child to be harmed. These dares are less about stunts, and more about personal growth, in whatever form that would help the child the most. I'm sorry you've had to rescue two people this week who were doing things they shouldn't have, but that has nothing to do with my program."

I leaned forward as far as I could. "Two people are in the hospital, Hessa."

She jumped up, anger spotting her cheeks, those brown eyes flashing. "And I'm sorry about that. But show me the evidence. How are they connected to my program?"

I sat back, unable to provide that for her, realizing this conversation had gone way off course. I'd guessed she was devoted to her students, but I underestimated her passion.

She crossed her arms over her chest. "I see. You have no evidence. Then I can't help you. I wish you luck, and I hope no more foolishness requires your aid."

And with that, I was thoroughly dismissed.

I stood slowly, if only to irritate her further. I stood directly in front of her, my face only inches from hers. I liked her passion. I didn't like that she clammed up on me, or chose to argue with me, but her passion excited me on a fundamental level. What is life without passion?

"Do all your male students have crushes on you, Ms. Woodland?"

She gasped and I smiled, picturing her clutching a pearl necklace had she been wearing one, so great was her indignation.

"I didn't take you for a blackguard, Mr. Kāne."

I shook my head, refusing to be distracted by her fancy words.

"When you're ready to talk to me about this without shutting me down immediately, you know where to find me. I don't wish to accuse you. I came here today to understand it." In parting, I traced my finger down her arm, wanting a feel of that soft skin again, getting an even better reaction when I saw her shiver.

I smiled and walked out.

I'd never had such a wonderful time at high school before.

Hessa

I'd never been so happy to see someone leave my classroom. One, because he was accusatory and I didn't appreciate that. Two, because he was purposely trying to rile me up with that comment and that touching. Three, because I got to admire his backside as he walked away from me. And what a backside it was.

Once my heart rate had returned to normal, I sat back down and grabbed the file out of my drawer. The one I'd been digging for when he came in my classroom. In it, I had all the current Care Dares my seniors had submitted. I flipped through each one as I sat there, looking for any dare that might involve the ocean. So far, only two had anything to do with water and the dares had only been submitted. They hadn't been approved by me, nor had the students acted on them, to the best of my knowledge.

I wrote the two names on a Post-it and made a note to talk to them tomorrow. I wanted to make sure they hadn't taken the dares into their own hands. I scoffed at the idea, but if there was even a small doubt in my mind, I wanted to lay it to rest.

I didn't recall Kai telling me what the ages were of the two people he'd rescued. Damn. I should have asked him. But I could hardly be expected to think of appropriate questions when he was in the room. Or talking to me. Or looking at me like that with those mesmerizing hazel eyes.

And now I was supposed to meet Esa and Bailey at Chocolate Dreams. What if Kai showed up? We'd just had an argument, for cripes' sake! How awkward would that be?

Aha! I'd just run in, grab a hot chocolate and go. Tell Esa all about it later.

I jumped up, grabbed my bag loaded down with papers to grade and headed out.

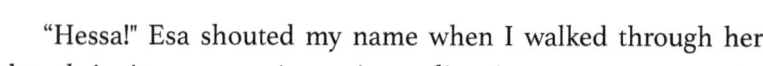

"Hessa!" Esa shouted my name when I walked through her door, bringing everyone's eyes in my direction.

Welp, there went my idea of just running in and back out without anyone noticing me. I waved to her over at a table with a crew of lifeguards and walked in the other direction to the counter to place my order.

Before I could figure out what I wanted, Esa hollered over to me again. "Hessa, wait! Come over here and try my newest flavor before you order." I grimaced before pasting a smile on my face and turning around. She was only trying to be helpful by coming up with a way for me to join their little group. Kai was two seats over from her, skewering me with his stare. I resolutely ignored him and sauntered over to their group like I had all the time in the world and all the reason to be there.

"Jax, give up your seat, would ya'? Everyone, this is my friend Hessa." Esa practically pushed poor Jax off his chair, which was of course, situated right next to Kai. I gave Esa a quick hug and then maneuvered my way to the now empty chair. The spacing was tight and I had to shimmy between the chairs, putting my ample ass in Kai's face to get the job done. I begged the gods to keep the blush from my cheeks for as long as it took to get out of this situation.

The lifeguards around the table all said their hellos and I caught a few names but didn't retain any of them. Too much testosterone in one place, along with the feel of Kai's stare burning into my skin, scrambled my brain.

"Hessa." Kai merely said my name and the trembling in my body started. "Lovely to see you again."

In slow motion, I turned my head in his direction, almost jumping when I realized my thigh was practically sitting on his lap. Could the chairs be any closer? Or my thigh be any wider?

"Kai." I gave my well-practiced head nod and looked away. I managed one word, maybe I could go for two next time.

"Here, girlie. Try this new one I made today. It's chocolate praline." Esa interrupted my silent treatment by shoving her cup at me. I took the lifeline she offered and tipped the cup to my lips. The flavor was dark and nutty. I couldn't hold back a soft moan from escaping as I set her cup down on the table.

Kai reached across me, presenting his own cup. "Try this one. It's macadamia nut chocolate." His eyes were piercing green and laser focused on my lips. I kept my gaze on his face, intrigued by his focus. I took a quick sip, catching a drip of hot chocolate out the side of my mouth with my tongue.

Before I could let him know what I thought of the taste, he'd shoved his chair back. He reached down and pulled me up by my arm, dragging me over to the counter.

"Kai!" I was about to lose my footing in these damn heels and I didn't particularly like to be dragged anywhere.

He didn't stop, instead throwing me an intense look over his shoulder that shut me up. I didn't know what he was so mad about, but we were going to have words. Starting with a rule about no dragging, which shouldn't need to be stated.

When we reached the counter, he spun me around and backed me up till I had nowhere to go. His chest was brushing up against mine and I lost my train of thought. His hands landed on my hips and for one brief dream-like moment, he pulled my hips into contact with his. My breath lodged in my throat and I could have sworn I felt more than just two hip bones pressing into my belly.

Then he was spinning me around again, speaking to the clerk behind the counter. "She'll take the macadamia hot chocolate. Whip, Ono?" He whispered that last part in my ear. Only one part of my body still touched his. I was thankful, maybe for the first time, for my impressive derriere.

"Ono?" I squeaked out the word, too befuddled to process what he meant by that.

"It means 'delicious'. Did you want whipped cream, Hessa?" He pushed off the counter and headed back to the table, leaving me cold, confused and more than a little turned on.

The clerk was still looking at me, cup and marker in hand, waiting to see if I wanted whipped cream, I suppose. Her eyes were on Kai's back, however.

"No whip, please," I whispered.

"That was hot..." she whispered back, still not bothering to look my direction.

5

essa

I was relishing sleeping in on Saturday morning, knowing I had stacks of papers to grade, but enjoying just a moment longer in bed. My sheets were warm and cozy, my pillow inviting me to stay a little longer. But my brain was focused on replaying my encounters with Kai. All my awkwardness, his hot and cold treatment, his pet name for me. Ono, meaning delicious? Did that mean he thought I was tasty? Or he wanted to taste me? Or was he just teasing me? Call the fat girl delicious as she orders more sugary chocolate?

I tossed my sheets back and climbed out of bed in a huff. There was no use second-guessing things. I wasn't fat by any means. I was a size twelve for God's sake. That was smaller than the average American female. I wasn't overly self-conscious about my body and I wasn't going to let some muscled-up, tattoo-bearing, hazel-eyed lifeguard make me start doubting myself. So there.

With my attitude readjusted, I threw on some workout clothes and put my hair up in my standard ponytail. My doorbell went off, making me whip my head up from tying my tennis shoes. My pony whacked me in the eye and I hopped, one foot in a shoe, one barefoot, one eye squeezed shut and the other darting around. By some small miracle, I made it down the stairs and swung the door open.

My stinging eye became the least of my problems when I saw who'd darkened my door.

"Hessa."

"Rainna."

My sister. My twin sister. My twin sister who I hadn't spoken to in two years.

"May I come in?" She didn't smile and neither did I. But I did back up to let her step through the doorway.

You give her an inch, she'll take a mile, just like always. She waltzed right into my private space and helped herself to a seat on my couch.

"To what do I owe the pleasure of your company, dear sister?" I sat down on the chair next to the couch and crossed my arms over my chest. I couldn't imagine why she was here. We'd said all we needed to say two years ago when I'd loaned her money yet again, correct as usual that she'd piss it away with nothing to show for it. The break had been a peaceful one, even though I'd find myself about to call her and putting the phone back down again, heart dropping at the loss.

We'd been close growing up, until we'd hit puberty. I hadn't changed much but Rainna became a wild child. She cut her hair super short, dyed it crazy colors and body piercings started showing up in random locations. I resented these changes as I took them as a personal offense. She didn't want to look like me anymore and that hurt. Things got worse after high school when I went off to college and Rainna jumped from minimum wage job to minimum wage job, all while only contacting me when she needed financial help from the responsible sister. I'd grumble, I'd give lectures, but I'd always give her the money.

Until two years ago. For whatever reason, I'd snapped, refusing to give her a damn penny and kicking her out of my house. When I was done, I was done.

She was following in the footsteps of our father, completely abandoning responsibility and letting everyone else pick up the slack. I hadn't had a choice when I was just a kid. He'd left us with our mother, traveling in his van all over the country, never remembering to write us on our birthday or send child support checks. When we did see him, he'd laugh off our concerns, saying we needed to "chill". I hated everything about his hippie lifestyle and now as an adult, I had no intention of being involved with anyone like that again.

Now we sat, staring at each other, cataloguing the differences that two years can make. Rainna's hair was longer than mine and dark brown now. She looked thinner but in a healthy, fit way. A few more tattoos decorated her arms and several facial piercings were noticeably missing.

"You look good, Hessa."

I snorted in response. Her eyes dropped and I watched her square her shoulders to try again.

"It's been two years." She looked up at me and I thought I saw a confidence and clarity in her gaze that had never been there before.

"It has. How's life been?" I did want to know what she'd been up to since I saw her last. I may not approve of how she was living her life, or how she was trying to use me, but that didn't mean I'd stopped caring. She was my twin; I'd never stop caring.

Her eyes softened at my question and I felt like we were eight years old again, sharing secrets in our indoor tent made of blankets draped over chair backs.

"I've been really good, Hess. I'm part owner of a tattoo shop north of L.A. I'm saving for a down payment for a small house up there." She stopped and the corners of her mouth turned down. "But I miss you."

I closed my eyes, savoring her words. My heart melted and I wanted to believe her so badly. But part of me still wondered if she was buttering me up for an outrageous request. I hated that I expected that from her, but years of similar treatment trained me to think like that.

"I miss you too, Rain." That was honest and I could give her that.

"But you won't forgive me, is that it?" The hardness was back in her eyes, dousing the hope that flared.

"It's not a matter of forgiving you. I'll always forgive you, you know that. What I won't do is continue to let you, or anyone else, treat me badly." I was tired of having this conversation. Maybe one day it would get through her thick skull.

She closed her eyes, took a deep breath and continued. "I know. I know I treated you badly and I'm sorry. I can promise I won't treat you like that again. I'm getting my life together. Finally. I hope one day you'll come to trust me. Can you at least keep an open mind about me?"

I'm sure coming here and apologizing, for the first time ever, took a lot of courage. I didn't know what her angle was, but I could meet her halfway and promise to give her a second chance.

"Thank you for your apology. And yes, I'll try to lock down the negativity and keep an open mind." I nodded, confirming my commitment.

A smile formed on her face, transforming her from average woman to beautiful creature. I'd missed that smile, so open and free with unrestrained happiness.

I put my hand on hers, giving her a squeeze meant to convey forgiveness, hope, and love. A small gesture to signal the start of our long journey back.

She stood up, looking ready to head out. She glanced down at the ottoman in front of the couch and promptly sat back down.

Her hands shuffled the papers there, before grabbing them up in excitement.

"Are you writing a poem? A song?" She looked overly intrigued and I couldn't let her continue to read my inner most thoughts expressed on paper.

I snatched the papers out of her hands and held them to my chest. "Just playing around so I don't lose the plot dealing with teenagers all day."

She laughed, entertained by my attempt to cover my panic, I'm sure. "You're the last person who will ever 'lose the plot', Hessa. When you look up practicality in the dictionary, it pops up your picture," she said out of the side of her mouth, a wry smile in place.

"Exactly. That's why I write. To make sure I don't lose my mind. They say using both sides of your brain leads to a lower chance of mental decline later in life."

Rainna chuckled and walked to my front door. "I'm sure they do. See you soon?"

"Absolutely."

Kai

"Have you heard anything about an online dare or challenge game?" I was sitting on the beach, stretching to prepare for my run. After my disastrous talk with Hessa, I'd decided to call Jack, a detective at HB Police. I had that feeling in the pit of my stomach that something was off. It may have nothing to do with Hessa's Care Dare, but I'd bet my life there was something organized going on, causing these people to attempt dangerous stunts. It wouldn't hurt to call Jack and rope him in on it. As a precaution.

"Hmm. I don't think so, off the top of my head. Would you

give me more information on what you're talking about?" Jack's voice came through the phone dead serious.

I gave him the quick version on the two saves I'd made, the wording that they used, and my suspicions about Hessa's program.

"Isn't that Bailey and Esa's new friend? The school teacher?" Jack's voice perked up.

"I think so. Wait, are they friends?" I was confused. I figured they knew each other, but friends? The woman drove me crazy in the best and worst of ways. I wasn't sure I could handle seeing her at all our group gatherings. Esa took her Beach Squad seriously. If she wanted Hessa, that girl was as good as branded.

"Yeah, I think so. Bailey was talking about their shopping trip the other day and they're planning on getting together today to run on the beach. I assumed that meant they were friends. But those girls are crazy, your guess is as good as mine. They do what they want and I'm sure they'll tell us about it later when it suits them." Jack sounded about as frustrated as I was.

Time to move the conversation on so I could get to my run and burn off my frustration. "Okay, well let me know if you hear anything about these dares. If anything else comes up on my end, I'll give you the heads-up."

"Sounds good, brother. Be safe."

I turned my phone off, stashed it in my glove box and locked my truck. I was about to walk over to the cement walkway when I spotted a gaggle of women walking on the sand down by the water. Based on the volume and cackling, it was easy to see it was the very women Jack and I were discussing.

My eyes sought out Hessa, finding her in the middle of the pack, that blonde hair up in a ponytail swinging in the wind as they walked. My gaze traveled downward, taking in the sway of those hips, the ones I'd had my hands on for too brief a moment the other night.

The sound of her laughter carried over and I could barely

control my body from moving toward her. It was like every cell in my body knew I needed to be near her, while my head didn't want anything to do with another argument with her. I had always enjoyed peace and quiet, and I experienced anything but that when I was with her.

With that reminder in my head, I spun around and began jogging the opposite way. She was the most beautiful woman I'd ever seen and she was getting under my skin, but she wasn't for me.

Hessa

Today was turning out to be the oddest day ever. It started with my sister's unexpected visit and all the emotions that churned up. Then I'd gotten a text from Bailey, inviting me to join her and her friends at the beach for a jog. I'd tried to let her know there was no 'I' in jogging, before I realized there actually was one, and she insisted I come. It was the promise of frequent walking breaks and brunch afterwards that lured me in. Getting further intel on Kai from the ladies wasn't part of the decision process at all. Nope.

When I'd arrived, I realized the Beach Squad, as they called themselves, consisted of quite a few ladies. I'd met Bailey and Esa, of course, but I was also introduced to Brinley, the most stunning specimen of a woman I'd ever seen. Then there was Shasta, a pretty, middle-aged woman who owned a self-defense studio here in HB. And Autumn, who had these legs that were so gorgeous I wanted to take a picture of them as a physical example of perfection.

"Ladies, I must tell you, I don't jog much. Like at all. So, if you need to leave me, just run ahead. I'll take no offense." I was nervous surrounded by all these beauties, my self-confidence taking another hit.

"Yo, Hessa. I'm gonna lay this out straight away so there's no confusion. You're part of the Beach Squad now. We don't leave a woman behind. Period." Shasta laid a gentle hand on my shoulder, her fierce gaze telling me she wasn't joking.

I nodded. "Okay, got it." Hello, intimidating.

"I doubt you do, but you'll catch on." Shasta squeezed my shoulder and gave me a warm smile.

We started up at a slow jog pace, Autumn and Brinley leading the pack with entertaining stories about swimsuit malfunctions during volleyball games. I didn't say a word; I just focused on putting one foot in front of the other and not making a fool of myself.

Just when I thought my lungs might actually catch on fire with all the burning that was going on, Bailey called for a break. We slowed to a walk and my calves begged me to give it up already. I figured out how Autumn got those legs and I wanted no part of it. Perfection was overrated.

"Ready to pick it up again?" Brinley called out, enthusiasm dripping from every word.

"For the love..." I muttered. Esa shot me a sympathetic look.

I limped along in the back, cursing myself for ever meeting these girls. Cursing the cell phone that delivered the text inviting me here. Cursing my decision to locate to HB where these sadists lived. Why did the sand shift and give me nothing to push off of? Why did the beach go on for so long? Why were we running when society had invented automobiles, therefore negating the need for physical exertion?

Finally, the burning and huffing and puffing was so bad I had to tap out. "Sorry--girls--I can't--go--any further," I gasped out, stopping to stoop over and gulp in oxygen.

The girls all stopped and gathered around me. "No worries,

girlie. I was wanting a break too. Why don't you catch your breath and we'll just walk?" Esa was sweet to offer me an out.

I looked up at them and realized no one else looked like they were about to pass out. "How the hell do you all do it? Am I really that out of shape? I can't drag my fat ass for a paltry mile run?" It was depressing. I'd be embarrassed later, once I was reassured I'd survive this torture.

"Oh hell, no." Bailey pushed her way in front of me, dragging me back up to standing. "Not one of us has a fat ass around here, and even if we did, we'd celebrate that thing. Bad asses come in all shapes and sizes, my dear. And speaking of asses. If you continue to throw shade at yours, I will kick your ass. You got me?"

"Um..."

"Leave the girl alone, B. You're scaring her." Esa wedged in and drew my attention away from Bailey. "What she's trying to say is that we're all about loving our bodies around here. We love their shapes, sizes, and quirks. We still work to be as healthy as we can, but we let go of any shame about our physical selves. Life's too short for that shit, you know?"

Shasta interjected. "You're Beach Squad now. We're a group of women who truly believe in ourselves as human beings, not just as women. We don't impose society's beauty rules on ourselves. We recognize and create our own beauty, no matter what form it comes in. We don't care to shrink down smaller. We strive to live big. We have more to offer than six-pack abs or a booty that don't stop. And I bet you do too."

I blinked. A wave crashed onto the sand, spraying mist up into the air. A seagull swooped low over our heads and skimmed the water. A child ran screaming from the water into her parent's arms. I took it all in and let it swirl through my brain. These women, those words.

It was like a calming wave of empowerment filled up my chest cavity, leaving my heart on fire and my brain at rest. The bitch voice in my head was silent for the first time since puberty. I didn't know exercise endorphins were this intense, but maybe I'd be doing more jogging if I could feel like this again.

I began softly, my voice gaining confidence as I laid it all out there. "I felt like a fish out of water when we first started our jog. Now I know for sure I've found my tribe. You ladies are a gift and I'm blessed to be part of your group." I gave a big smile to each of them. "Thanks for pulling my head out of my fabulous ass."

"Now that's what I'm talkin' 'bout!" Bailey pulled me into a hug, then sent me down the line to hug everyone else.

I woke bright and early Monday morning, getting ready for another day teaching the bright minds of our youth. I took extra time to wear one of my new outfits picked out by Bailey, enjoying the way the tailored skirt and shirt fit my body, confident in all my curves.

When I bustled onto campus, I went straight to my classroom to make a list of which students still needed to turn in their dare approval sheets. Ten minutes before the first bell rang, my door swung open and a group of students rushed in all talking at once.

"Slow down, guys. One at a time, tell me what's going on." I held my hands up, trying to bring the excitement level down a few notches.

"Ms. Woodland. Is it true? Are you going to do the dare too?" This question came from Alessa, a bright girl in my third period English class.

"Me? Do a dare? No. That's definitely not on the table." I chuckled, wondering what she was thinking.

"But you've been dared already! Are you saying you won't do it?" Josh piped in, looking confused.

I furrowed my brow, trying to piece together what he as

talking about. "I don't know what you mean, Josh. I haven't been dared."

"Yes, you have. See?" Alessa held up her iPhone, showing my own Instabook page.

The top cover photo was gone. In its place was one sentence: *I DARE you, Hessa Woodland: sing one of your songs publicly. #CAREDARE*

6

---

he blood drained from my face and my vision narrowed till all I saw was that dare staring at me, mocking me from behind a glass screen. My mind went blank and I didn't even hear the bell ring nor see the kids that rushed to take their seats. I had that horrible buzz filling my head, that feeling when you know something is horribly off and absolutely nothing good could come of this thing.

The only reason I had an Instabook account was so I could monitor the Care Dares the kids were posting about each year. They were allowed to post about it as long as they used the appropriate hashtags so school administrators and parents could follow along.

Who could have done this? Why did someone do this? Who the hell even knew I wrote songs?

"Ms. Woodland? You want us to start reading the next chapter?" The voice of my student from the first row broke into my thoughts and reminded me I had a class to teach. Get through the next four classes, then I could take my lunch break and take the first steps to figuring out what was going on.

When I sat down in the teacher's lounge, I grabbed my phone and logged into my Instabook account.

Login Failed. Please try again.

I tried three more times before I realized I wasn't going to get in. My account had been hacked, that's for sure. I created a new user account and went to my old account, reviewing the dare again. Nothing further was posted on my account, but I took a screenshot of what was there.

Then I went to the Care Dare hashtags and reviewed what the kids were posting. Since their own dares hadn't even started yet, they were mostly talking about me. Lots of speculation on who dared me and what the song thing was all about. One post even went so far as to say I was a famous singer, teaching incognito for kicks. Ha! Like a millionaire singer would teach high school English in their spare time just for fun. Perhaps my kids had a different idea of 'fun'.

I sobered quickly when I remembered the issues Kai was having. Two of his saves had mentioned being dared. It didn't have to do with my program, but I was starting to wonder what was going on since something, or someone, outside of my program had now dared me.

I thought of at least ten reasons why I shouldn't contact Kai, but in the end, my practicality won out. If my dare had anything to do with what he thought might be going on, it would be a smart move to at least let him know. And I wanted to know if he'd found out anything further. I could survive a conversation, I was sure of it.

I had my phone in hand, ready to dial the lifeguard headquarters, when I got a text from my sister.

Rainna: *Had a nice time chatting the other day. You should come see my shop soon. Xoxo*

I covered my mouth, eyes wide. My estranged sister was at my house just two days ago and saw my songwriting. Today, I get dared publicly to sing one of my songs. Coincidence? I didn't think so.

Hessa: *Very funny stunt you pulled. How about you give me back my hacked account now?*

Rainna: *??*

Tessa: *Just be honest. Did you hack my Instabook account?*

Rainna: *Hell, no. I don't do social media.*

And that left me back where I started, if I trusted Rainna when she said she didn't do it. Which I didn't.

I sighed, the inevitable chafing my skin like an ill-fitting, cheap thong. I'd have to call Kai. I dialed the number listed on the City of Huntington Beach website and waited through four rings, reminding me of a rhythmic death march to my humiliation.

"Lifeguard Headquarters. How can I help you?" A perky woman answered the phone and I prayed I could leave a voicemail.

"Hello. I'm trying to reach Kai Kāne. Can you help me with that?"

"Sure, let me transfer you. If he's available, he'll answer, otherwise just leave a message."

A peppy Beach Boys song came on while I waited on hold. I'd met the lead singer at a fundraiser one time. I high-fived him...my claim to fame.

Voicemail, voicemail, voicemail... I chanted my wish, throwing it out to the universe to take care of for me.

"Kai Kāne, how can I help you?"

Dammit, universe.

"Uh, hi, Kai." Now I was rhyming. This was not starting off well. "This is Hessa Woodland."

There was a pause. I wondered if I should clarify who I was. Would he have forgotten?

"Hessa." He paused. "How did you like that macadamia hot chocolate?" His voice had deepened, gotten more intimate.

Oh, he knew who I was.

"It was quite delicious." Oh Lord, did I really bring that up again? I wanted to forget he'd called me 'ono' even though I'd been reliving that moment for several nights in a row as I went to sleep at night.

He chuckled, the sound warm and friendly. "I'm sure it was delicious. Not that you need a reason, but what are you calling for this lovely Monday?"

"Well, I'm not sure. I had something odd happen today and I think it may be connected to those dares you were talking to me about. It could also just be my semi-criminal sister having a joke on me. But I didn't want to take any chances. I'm on my lunch break right now and have to get back to class shortly. Do you have time to talk later today?" I forced my hands to stop pulling on my sweater. We were simply two professionals talking. No need to flutter around like a scared school girl on her first date.

"It must be serious if you're calling me, admitting there might be some validity to what I was asking you about." I could practically hear the smirk on his face. "How about you come down to the beach after I get off at five. Meet me at Headquarters and wear workout clothes. That work for you?"

I sputtered. "Focus your audio. If I'm wrong, I have no problem saying I'm wrong. I just thought you might be interested in what transpired today because it might be connected. No need to bring the snark." What was it about this guy that made me defensive in two seconds flat?

"Hessa, I meant no offense. I'm going to assume that calling me a week after arguing how there could be no possible connection to your program would be a hard call to make. That makes me think you have something very serious to discuss. There's no time to waste. So. Five o'clock, Headquarters. You good?"

I sighed. Maybe I was a bit defensive. I felt like I needed his help so I'd have to suck it up, buttercup. "Okay. I'll be there. Wait-- why am I wearing workout clothes?"

"See you soon, Hessa." Click.

That aggravating man! I needed his help, but this seemed too steep a price to pay.

Even so, my traitorous heart skipped a beat as it counted the minutes until our meeting.

It was a rush, but I stopped by my house to change and still made it to Lifeguard Headquarters in time to meet Kai at five o'clock. I was a stickler for punctuality and he didn't disappoint. He was standing outside the front door, spotting me as I pulled into the parking lot. He came over and opened my car door for me, which spoke to my heart, a sentimental lover of all things chivalrous and old fashioned.

"Kai." I stood, tugging my shirt down, trying to cover the glorious ass that was on display in these tight workout pants. Time to practice my self-love, a' la Beach Squad.

"Hessa." He put a hand on my lower back and steered me down the ramp leading to the beach. "Let's stretch."

We sat down on a cement half wall and he proceeded to put me through a series of stretches.

"Did you forget your shoes?" I asked, not hiding the snark in my tone. The man was barefoot, which seemed weird when everyone around us had on either flip-flops or tennis shoes.

"No." He didn't seem perturbed by my question at all. In fact, his smirk seemed to speak volumes, mocking me for being the one in footwear.

"What are we doing here?" I had a bad feeling about this. Anything that required this much stretching was bound to be a level of strenuous beyond my capabilities.

"This is what I do after work most days of the week. I go for a run. Today, you get to join me." Kai actually gave me a look that was supposed to be magnanimous, but little did he know I had no intention of taking him up on this running 'gift'.

"Oh, I'm not a runner. How about I stay here and grade some papers while you go on your run? We'll talk after."

"Hessa." He glared at me with a hint of a smile, like I was a petulant child who would change her mind.

"Kai." I put my hands on my hips and stood my ground. I was still recovering from shin splints from my run with the Beach Squad two days ago. I wasn't doing that again.

"We'll go slow. Take breaks. You'll love it." He lost the glare and smiled at me instead, showing off that dimple. The dimple with powers over my cognitive ability.

"We better check the weather report. I think it's supposed to rain this evening." My excuses were getting weak, but a girl had to try, right?

Kai spread his hands out, palms up, tipping his head back and scanning the sky. "Look up. Check out that blue sky. See any dark clouds?"

"Well, I don't see them right now, but the weather report said--"

"Hessa. We don't need a little app to tell us what the weather is. Just take a look outside. Don't let that app control your life." Kai stepped closer and cupped my face with his two hands, tilting my head back, forcing me to look up at the clear blue sky.

"Hmm..." I wasn't sure if I was commenting on the sky or merely moaning my appreciation of his hands on my face.

He brought my face back to meet his gaze, thumb sweeping back and forth across my cheek. He had a patient smile and his eyes had gone soft. "Come with me, Ono," he whispered.

It was the whispered nickname that threw all my excuses out the window. When one quietly spoken word can make your stomach melt and your heart glow, you shouldn't fight it. I'd never felt this way before and I was curious and tempted enough to go with it to see where it would lead.

I nodded my acceptance, earning me another dimpled smile. I burned that look into my brain to help me endure the next thirty minutes of torture. When his hand slid away from my face and grabbed ahold of my hand, I was ready to sign up to do this every day.

We walked out onto the sand, just steps away from the retreating water's edge. He kept his hand around mine, swinging our joined arms as we walked. True to his word, we never ran, just walked in comfortable silence, taking in the peacefulness of the beach at this hour. Only a few people were out enjoying this paradise. The sun was close to setting and I wondered if we looked like a couple in love, going for a romantic walk on the beach. The thought was more appealing than I would ever admit.

"So, you wanna tell me what's going on? What's got you worried?" Kai broke the silence, giving me an encouraging look.

I shook myself out of my love-sick daydream and focused on what I came here for. "Let me just preface this by saying I don't think what I have to tell you has anything to do with my program, but in case it does, I wanted to be on the safe side." I looked over at him out of the corner of my eye to see him nodding that he understood. "When I got to school this morning, some of my students ran in and showed me my account on Instabook. My profile had been hacked and my cover photo was now a dare, just for me. I've been dared to sing one of my songs in public."

Kai looked concerned. He pulled us to a stop and faced me, letting go of my hand to fold his arms over his chest. "You have no idea who could have done that?"

"No. I mean, it may have been my sister, but she denied it when I asked today."

"Why do you think your sister would have done it?"

"Well, she and I don't have the best relationship in recent years and she was just at my house on Saturday and carelessly, I had my songs out. I thought maybe she was just being an obnoxious cow. But she didn't seem to know anything about it when I asked her."

"Who else knows you write songs?"

"No one! That's the whole thing. I write for the fun of it. It's like a quiet little hobby of mine that I don't share with anyone. I let out my stress or anger or sadness, or any emotion really, by putting it all down on paper in song form. It's highly personal. And now the whole world knows I write songs!" I was wringing my hands, shifting from side to side, wanting to outrun the discombobulating situation.

Kai grabbed my hands in his and pulled me down onto the sand. We sat facing the ocean and I wondered what we were doing.

"When I'm stressed, I like to run on the beach and then meditate as the sun sets. It's become a habit of mine that keeps me centered and focused on the things that matter. Close your eyes." Kai closed his eyes too, but kept his hand on my thigh, our knees touching.

The conversation had veered off into a direction I wasn't anticipating, but I went with it as I seemed to be unable to say no to this man. I looked around and saw that no one was in our immediate vicinity which lowered my chance of being caught looking like a hippie-dippy meditating in public. Kai squeezed my thigh, causing me to jump and then follow directions by closing my eyes.

"Take a deep breath in. And blow it out. Good. Another deep breath. Focus on filling your lungs and then exhaling all the air." Kai was speaking in a low, soothing tone. My body was following his instructions and I found myself relaxing my shoulders down, the panic leaving my body as if sucked out by the ocean breeze.

"Now just keep breathing deep and allow your mind to drift. Feel the sand on your legs, the wind in your hair, the sound of the waves crashing. Feel all that the universe has given you. Breathe in the energy of the universe, exhale the stress we've placed on ourselves." Kai's voice drifted off, leaving me to continue my breathing.

As much as I wanted to laugh at this silliness, it was working. I felt like that one time at a faculty party when I'd downed a whole glass of champagne and the room had gone pleasantly fuzzy. My limbs felt detached from my body, my head floated up in the clouds, and I'd forgotten what I was talking about earlier. The heat from the delectable man next to me kept me from completely losing touch with my surroundings.

I couldn't tell how long we sat there, just absorbing the present moment, but when Kai squeezed my knee sometime later, I wasn't ready to leave that calm cocoon. I could feel his stare on my face, but even then I didn't open my eyes. I didn't want to return to heated conversations that left me tongue-tied, a world where my private habit was publicly exposed, or a place where people were wrecking the great reputation of the Care Dare program.

I don't know how long meditation experts sat in contemplation but I was willing to run for the Guinness Book of World Records.

"Let's get you back, Ono," Kai whispered to me.

I peeped one eye open. He hopped up and held out his hand. I let out a most pathetic sigh and let him help me up. He kept ahold of my hand while walking us back in the direction of the Headquarters building.

"Got plans Wednesday?" Kai wasn't looking at me and the question seemed casual enough.

"No, I don't believe I do." I reserved my enthusiasm since conversations with Kai rarely went down a normal path.

"Meet me here again at five. We'll step things up to a slow jog and do the meditation thing again. I think you like it." He winked at me before continuing. "In the meantime, I'll call my friend Jack, a police detective, and see if he has anything else about these dares. I'll need your phone number in case anything else comes up."

Smooth. That was real smooth.

"Why, Mr. Kāne. Did you just request my phone number?" I had my hand over my heart and the most innocent of shocked expressions on my face.

"Don't get excited, Ms. Woodland. I ask for all the hot English teacher's phone numbers." He smirked at me in response.

He could pretty much do anything right then and I wouldn't argue. The hottie lifeguard just called <u>me</u> hot. We exchanged numbers and I left, the tranquility from the meditation and Kai's deep voice carrying me all the way home.

Kai

I watched Hessa drive away, more unsure of what I was doing than ever. I told myself I'd stay away from her, but everywhere I turned, there she was.

They sure hadn't made high school English teachers like her when I was going to school. The sexy librarian look of skirts and heels and glasses. And then tonight, the tight pants that high-lighted that ass of hers. I wanted to grab it, squeeze it, and hang a sign on it claiming it as mine.

Just when I thought I had her figured out, she showed me another side to her. She used brainiac words I'd never heard of, acting superior looking down her nose at us normal people. But then she melted into the sand enjoying the meditation more than I did. She argued with me and got defensive over every little thing I said, but then she'd told me she wrote songs and was embar-rassed for anyone to find out.

I realized I was trying to pigeonhole her. Trying to fit her in a nice tidy box so I could understand her, reject her, and stay in my conformable little life. I hated when people did that, having been the pigeon shoved into that hole more times than I could count in my life. People had certain stereotypes in mind when you were born and raised in Hawaii.

I sighed, rubbing my hands along my cheeks, trying to clear my head of all things Hessa. I needed to put my personal feelings, as conflicted as they were, aside and focus on what was happening in my town. Someone was daring people to do reckless things and I needed to put a stop to it.

I dialed Jack's number from inside my truck. I hoped I wasn't bothering him so late in the evening, but he said to contact him immediately if anything else happened.

"Kai. What's up, man?" Jack seemed less serious than usual. I was about to ask if I was calling at a bad time when I heard a female voice laughing in the background. Clearly, I was interrupting.

"Sorry to interrupt. I'll keep this short."

"No problem at all." I heard a door slam shut and it got significantly quieter on his end of the line. "What's happening?

"You know the teacher at Surf City High that coordinates the Care Dare program we talked about? She told me she got dared this morning. Someone hacked into her social media account and dared her publicly. It's not a dangerous dare, but it is something not too many people know about and she wishes would have remained private. She's starting to wonder if it's connected to the two saves I had last week." I had no evidence to go off of, just a gut feeling that they were connected and part of something bigger.

"Hmm. That's definitely interesting. My tech guy notified me today that he's found some chatter about dares online in the area. HBPD got called out on a train jumper the other day. He got across the tracks before the train hit him, but he must have dropped something that messed with the tracks. Crew had to come out and fix it. They haven't found who did it, but we found the dare online. My tech guy's trying to trace it, but the IPs keep leading nowhere. I'd tell your friend to sit tight and don't engage if he reaches out and contacts her further."

The giggling female was back, telling Jack to hurry up. A little less giggle this time and more sass.

"Sorry, Kai. I'll call you back tomorrow, okay?"

"Sure--"

But Jack had already hung up on me. Guess I'd hang up on me too if I had an eager woman waiting for me. Which of course, just brought me back to thinking of Hessa. I wondered what her giggle sounded like. Did she actually giggle? Or was that too juvenile for her? I'd love to hear her full out laugh. Something told me it would be quite the site to see her let go of her highbrow decorum.

 essa

Tuesday was a hellish day of questions from my students regarding my mystery dare. I explained over and over again that a dare from outside the program, not endorsed by the program, was not acceptable. There were rules and checks in place in the program so that dares were handled responsibly. I would not be engaging with my mystery dare partner. Period.

By last period, I was sure I'd have a mutiny on my hands soon. My students were hell-bent on making me see their side of the situation. If they had to stretch out of their comfort zones by their dares, I should have to also. The whole point of Care Dare was to stretch yourself and do something that was previously thought beyond your limits. To their minds, my song writing, something I never spoke of before, was perfect for a dare.

I did see their point, but beyond my fear of publicly singing my songs, I didn't feel comfortable being forced into something by a masked instigator hiding behind his or her keyboard. It was like a terror negotiation and they always say not to give in to negotiating. So there I'd stand, not giving in, but also facing the wrath of my students who felt I was holding myself to a different standard, one that had the luxury of not choosing to face fears in the form of dares. Never mind the fact that I was a teacher, not a student and therefore exempt from the dares.

A headache was brewing and I was as joyous as my students to hear the bell ring, signaling the end of the school day. All I wanted was peace and quiet. And my e-reader loaded with a good RomCom to transport me to another place, where Happy Ever Afters were guaranteed.

I jammed all my papers to grade in my tote bag and started the long trek to my car. My phone rang from somewhere in the depths of my bag. I placed my dirty travel coffee mug on my car's trunk. I rummaged around at the bottom of the bag, finally snagging the phone. I dropped my keys as I swiped to answer it before it quit ringing. I was a mess.

"Hello?" Damn, I should have checked who was calling before answering. It could have been my father, needing money from wherever he happened to be in that death trap of an RV he lived in.

"Hessa? It's Bailey. You okay?"

"Yes, hi. Sorry, dropped my keys when I answered the phone. What's up?" I swung my hefty bag onto the back seat and dropped into the driver's seat, immediately propping the phone in the crook of my neck to reach down and take my heels off. I was hoping to get feeling back in my toes sooner rather than later.

"I heard about you being dared to sing. I thought Esa and I should swing by and talk to you about it. You got plans tonight?"

"Um. No." Wait, how did she hear about it? And why did they want to talk about it?

"Okay, great. We'll be over around seven with food. You like sushi?"

"Yeah, sushi is great."

"See you soon then!" Bailey hung up on me before I even gave her my home address.

I was on my second glass of wine, which was unusual on any night, but especially on a school night. But saying no to the twin hurricane that was Bailey and Esa was nearly impossible. The sushi went down easy and I found the company stellar. I was finally seeing the benefit of being part of the Beach Squad. It wasn't all running on the beach till you thought you'd puke your guts out. It was also drinking wine and talking about anything and everything with friends who understood.

Esa dropped her voice way down deep to imitate Ivan, "No babe, we can't have a pig carry the rings down the aisle." Bailey and I cracked up laughing. She continued in her normal voice. "But they're so cute! Have you seen the micro pigs? I don't understand why he doesn't want that at our wedding." Esa was pouting and I felt for her, but I kinda saw where Ivan was coming from. There's a time and place for pigs and I didn't think a wedding on the beach was the right one.

"Oh girl, you gotta let that shit go. There's no pig, micro or otherwise, that's gonna hoof it through the sand to deliver your ring. Just be normal for once and borrow someone's kid to use as ring bearer." Bailey, shockingly, was the voice of reason.

"Aha! I know! How about a tortoise?" Esa jumped up from the couch, thinking her idea was the perfect solution. "I mean, they're made to trek through sand!"

Bailey and I cracked up again. This was going from bad to worse. I had to stop her and the wine in my system was going to help. "You know how slow a tortoise is, right? You'd have to start it down the aisle before you even start your vows, just to get it there in time. What if it stops to nibble on someone's dress? Or worse, takes a shit in the middle of your wedding. I love you, Esa, but you're a blithering idiot right now, fueled solely by that third glass of wine."

Esa shot me a frown, crossing her arms and sitting back down in a huff.

"While Esa gets over her snit, why don't you update us on the singing thing?" Bailey put her glass down on the coffee table, leaning closer to make sure she got the full scoop.

I sighed. Hopefully this would go better than when I talked to my students about it. I brought them up to speed on the social media hacking, the dare, and my arguments with my students.

"Ah, that's a rough situation you've been put in, Hess." Bailey looked sympathetic. Esa had dropped the pout and was now wrapped up in my predicament.

"I think you should totally do it!" Esa was back to clapping her hands and bouncing on my couch. "Practice on us. Sing a song."

"Oh no. I'm not singing in public or for you. You guys, this is so crazy private. No one was even supposed to know I wrote songs! I write as a way to process my feelings. It's an outlet for me that was never supposed to be public." Now I was the one pouting.

"So you've never shown anyone your songs?" Esa asked, mouth dropped open.

"No!"

"Wait, is it the singing or the song writing you like?" Bailey asked.

"Mostly the song writing. The singing is just what I do to make sure the melody works with the lyrics."

"So you've never tried to sell your songs?" Esa was having a hard time wrapping her brain around this just being a stress relief habit. To her, everything was a great new business idea.

"Well, no. Not really. I mean, it would be cool if someone thought they were good enough to buy, but no. It's mainly just for me."

"I don't know...I think your students have a point. You're scared to share your songs publicly, which is why daring you to do it was genius. But I have a question: if no one knows you write songs, how did this mystery person know to dare you to do it?" Bailey was as confused as I was.

"I don't know and that's what's freaking me out! I thought it might be my sister, but she said it wasn't her. Maybe they not only hacked my social media account but my cloud account too? That's where I keep my finished songs." I was getting worried again. If they'd hacked into my computer, I had bigger problems than just the dare.

"You better change all your passwords and check your accounts, just in case." Bailey lifted an eyebrow. "Come on, Hessa. Just sing us one song. Pretty please?" She clasped her hands together and looked like she was ready to beg.

Then Esa joined in, both of them giving me the most ridiculous puppy dog eyes, designed to weaken my resolve.

"Nooooo!" I jumped up to clear our plates. "Discussion over! Not gonna happen. No way. I'll be wearing a pine overcoat before that happens."

Bailey looked at Esa. "Is that one of your weird, mixed-up phrases?"

I interrupted, yelling over my shoulder as I went into the kitchen, "It means, over my dead body!"

Bailey shouted back at me. "Well, that's a little extreme. We should talk about why you have such low self-confidence, Hessa-girl. I bet your songs are beautiful and you're just too scared to share your brilliance with the world. I think you're being selfish and you don't even know it."

I popped back out of the kitchen to see that Bailey was dead serious. I opened my mouth to respond, but nothing came out. Ouch. No beating around the bush there.

"Time for us to go. Thanks for having us over." Esa jumped up and rushed Bailey to the front door, giving me an apologetic smile.

"Think about it..." Bailey called over her shoulder as Esa pushed her out the door. A trickle of shame climbed up my spine, like she'd seen something deep within myself I didn't want to acknowledge.

I was also back to wondering if I even wanted to be part of the Beach Squad.

I was three chapters into a new book on my e-reader, my eyes slowing losing focus when my phone rang. I glanced over at the clock on my bedside table, wondering who'd be calling at eleven o'clock on a Tuesday night. I remembered to look at the screen first this time and saw it was Rainna. A sense of dread filled my stomach, a leftover reaction I hoped would go away in time.

"Hello?" I answered, grogginess making my voice a little slurred.

"I know you're still up, so don't act like you've been asleep, missy." My sister's voice carried the smile I knew was on her face.

I grunted. "Hey, I'm a hard-core librocubularist. What's your excuse?"

She laughed. "I won't even ask what that means. I'm up because I'm a tattoo artist. We work late." Her voice lost the humor. "And I had a very interesting guy in my chair a few moments ago. You need to hear this."

"Oh no, give it to me." I sat up straighter in bed and pulled my covers higher, needing the warmth.

"This guy just came in for a tattoo as a walk-in tonight. He was chatting to me about some dare that he had to complete by this weekend. Something about cliff jumping in Newport. I wouldn't have normally paid any attention, but he specifically used the word 'dare' just like you texted me about. Is something going on?"

She sounded worried, which warmed my heart. I mean, I didn't want her upset on my account, but considering how long I'd gone thinking she didn't care about me at all, the concern felt nice.

"I'm not exactly sure, but I've got some friends looking into it for me. Are you sure you didn't hack into my Instabook page?"

Silence.

"Hessa. For the last time. No, I didn't hack into anything. I don't do the social media thing and I wouldn't do that to you. I wish you'd believe me." The concern in her voice was quickly turning to irritation.

I removed my glasses and rubbed my forehead. "I'm sorry. Really. I'm just at loose ends here and I don't know what's going on. I believe you and I won't doubt you again. Thank you for calling me and letting me know what you heard."

"If I hear anything else, I'll call you. Will you update me on what's going on so I know if you're okay?"

"You bet. Goodnight, Rainny-Day." I extended the olive branch in the form of our nicknames from when we were kids. The name felt rusty on my tongue. I couldn't remember the last time I called her that. Couldn't remember the last time I'd felt close enough to her to call her that.

"Goodnight, Hess-Mess."

Wednesday morning came and went. The conversation with my students about my dare dwindled as the day went on. I was confident that it would be practically forgotten by the time the weekend rolled around. I took a full, easy breath for the first time since Monday morning. I had hoped this would go away and life would return to normal.

My good mood might also have been something to do with a tan lifeguard meeting up with me tonight after work. There was something about his dimpled smile that lit me up from within. I wanted to see that smile, I wanted to be the reason he flashed that smile, and I wanted to bask in the glow of that happiness.

Mark my words, that smile was going into one of my songs.

I'd write a song about his physicality but that was the low hanging fruit that every rap song I'd ever had the misfortune to hear went for. Granted, I didn't listen to rap that often, but I doubted it had improved much over the years. The man was crazy hot. Looking at his body got me hot and bothered to the point of stumbling over my words and blushing furiously. My usual wit was lost somewhere between the muscles and the hazel eyes.

And even with all that starrifying my perception of him, he irritated me to no end. With his accusations about my program. With his lackadaisical attitude about life in general. With his conversations that left me off-kilter. He got under my skin, and I hadn't figured out if that was in a good way or not. The weakest parts of me decided I'd have to see him repeatedly to make a determination.

It was the same weak part of me that had me changing my clothes multiple times before I'd settled on another pair of tight black leggings topped with a sports bra that roped in the girls within an inch of their lives. If we were running tonight, these puppies weren't moving. I just hoped they continued to get blood flow while strapped into the industrial contraption. I redid my ponytail, making sure it didn't look like I'd been dragged through a bush backwards. I almost perked up my look with some lipstick, but I felt that might be over the top for running on the beach. Nothing says desperation like bright red lipstick while working out with a man.

When I reached Lifeguard Headquarters ten minutes early, Kai was already there waiting for me. He stood with his back leaning against the wall, one knee bent, foot on the wall, arms crossed over his chest. He was in a clean white polo shirt, accentuating his gorgeous skin tone. Reflective RayBans shielded his eyes from the sun and kept me from knowing where his eyes were looking as I swung into the parking lot. I noticed he was barefoot again and I wondered how he could stand the hot cement.

He appeared at my car door, giving me his hand as I exited, eliciting the same butterflies as before. He wasted no time leading me out onto to the sand.

"Ready to pick up the pace tonight?" He gave me a teasing smile, not yet indulging me with the dimples.

"Sure!" I needed to dial back the enthusiasm. That sounded entirely fake. No one would ever believe I was looking forward to running.

Kai laughed. "Don't worry. We'll just run for a little bit, then take a break. Plus I have a surprise for you after we're done."

"You think dangling that carrot out there like that will make me run faster?"

He shrugged. "It was worth a shot..."

"Come on, let's get this over with so I can get my surprise." I took off into a jog, headed north to the pier.

Kai caught up to me and kept me preoccupied by running right by the edge of the water, moving higher as each wave chased our feet. I had more to lose, being the only one in shoes. Before I knew it, we passed the pier and though my lungs were working overtime, my legs weren't on fire like last time I tried running.

"Time to slow it down, huh?" Kai didn't even sound like he was breathing hard.

Damn him.

We walked for another mile before turning around. Kai kept up the conversation telling stories about people he'd dealt with as his job as a lifeguard. I was now convinced there were some unhinged people hanging out at the beach. I thought high schoolers were hard to deal with, but that paled in comparison to what Kai had to deal with on a daily basis. I told him a few stories about my students and earned myself some flashes of that dimple.

By the time we'd reached our starting point, I was laughing and feeling totally comfortable around him. Irritation was nowhere to be found and I began to think I'd previously made it up.

"Okay, so sit here and start meditating while I go grab something out of my truck." Kai looked like a little boy eager to show off his prized possession. It was endearing.

"Go, go! I'll be fine." I plopped down on the sand and assumed the position. I closed my eyes and cleared my mind like he'd taught me to do last time.

Then I realized he was still there. I opened one eye to catch him staring at me. I waved him off, embarrassed to be sitting there meditating while he just watched me. He winked and took off, leaving me with a shy smile permanently affixed to my face.

Kai

Mission accomplished: I got the straight-laced Hessa to belly laugh, which was as awesome as I figured it would be. I felt like I'd won some hard-earned victory just getting her to let loose and be silly. She didn't seem at all pretentious now that the wall was down. I didn't know what was different today, but I felt like she was finally letting me see the real Hessa.

The physical attraction was there from the moment I saw her. Whether it was her prim and proper teacher attire or the yoga pants that molded to those long, curvy legs, I was undeniably attracted to her. I'd struggled all evening to keep my eyes off her breasts. I didn't know what the hell she was wearing underneath her tank top, but her breasts were pushed up and on display like they were on a platter for my personal feasting. I wanted to get my hands on her, taste her, see if we could be compatible physically, but I wasn't a twenty-year-old anymore, jumping on any girl who tempted me. I wanted more than sex. I wanted a life partner, a best friend. I needed to see if Hessa could be that person for me.

As well as things were going, I probably shouldn't bring her the surprise I was planning on. I was afraid pushing her buttons would make the fun-loving Hessa run and hide, leaving me with argumentative Ms. Woodland.

But I wanted to share part of myself with her, be vulnerable and see if she'd meet me halfway. I wasn't getting any younger and I knew what I wanted. Better to put things out there now and see if she'd run.

I grabbed my case out of the car and jogged back down to the sand, enjoying the sight of this beautiful woman enjoying a practice that had become an important part of my life. I sat down next to her, making sure my knee was against hers. If she was going to shut me down, I'd enjoy my last moments of touching her.

Hessa's eyes popped open, looking unfocused and relaxed. She smiled at me. With the backdrop of the sun dropping into the ocean like an orange fireball lighting up her blonde hair, she looked like an angel. I swear to God, my heart skipped a beat and I paused, knowing this was significant. There may have been a brick in my stomach, but there was also electricity pulsing through my body, making the world seem alive in technicolor. I knew I was curious and attracted before, but with that one look, I was hooked emotionally. I was all in, I had my heart in the game now.

I wanted her.

And just like that, I was nervous as hell. I second-guessed my next move, knowing it could push her too far, giving her permission to push me away.

"What is it, Kai?" Hessa's smile had morphed to a curious look, her eyes darting to my black case on the sand in front of us.

Time to jump and see if we'd fly. "I-I brought something that's really personal to me. It's something I grew up doing and I wanted to share it with you. See if you'd join me."

"Okay..."

That was the longest, drawn out 'okay' I'd ever heard. If I wasn't so nervous myself, I would have laughed at her reluctance.

Time to go for broke. "Without further ado..." I popped open the latch and threw back the lid. "I give you...my ukulele!"

I picked it up and brought it to my lap, fingers instantly finding their place, strumming a few bars out of habit.

Hessa's eyes opened wide and her smile grew. "That's fabulous! Let me hear you play!"

"Well, here's the thing. I know quite a few Hawaiian songs and some covers you'd probably recognize. But what I really want to do tonight is sing with you." I paused to make sure she understood my meaning and how badly I wanted this. "I want you to sing, Hessa."

essa

Crud muffin! He wanted me to sing!

Damn him and his persuasive abilities. He warmed me up with funny stories, got me all relaxed with meditation in front of nature's greatest show at eventide, and now he dropped this bomb on me.

The thing is, I really wanted to do it. But I was scared spitless to do it. And I hated that he put me on the spot like this. How could I say yes and overcome my fear in front of the person I wanted to impress most? How could I say no and risk hurting his feelings and pushing him away? For heaven's sake, he said it was highly personal, a part of his childhood, and he wanted to share it with me. Turning him down would be equivalent to a slap in the face.

Before I could even formulate an answer, tears sprang to my eyes. I was between a rock and a hard place. Either way I'd hurt someone: me or him.

"Whoa, hold on there. You don't have to do it. I want you to, but I won't pressure you further. I promise. Please don't cry." Kai tossed the ukulele back in its case and leaned over me, pulling my hands into his. Which of course, just made the tears fall faster.

He responded the only way an intelligent man can by pulling me into a hug, his warm arms wrapping me up, shielding me from the ocean breeze. Words would come later, but for now, this contact was everything I needed.

Coconuts and man-sweat.

His heavenly scent surrounded me and distracted me from my tears. My body melted into his, enjoying the feel of his muscles bracketing my form. I'd never been a small girl, but in his embrace, I felt protected by a force stronger and braver than me.

All too soon, he pulled back. His hands cupped my face and his thumbs wiped the tears off my cheeks.

"I'm sorry, Ono," he whispered, just inches from my lips.

I gave him my truth. "I want to. I'm just scared." It was a scared confession I hated to put words to, which wasn't what he wanted, but it was something. Something honest at least.

His hands never left my face, thumbs and gaze caressing my skin. "I know you're scared. But I know you'd be incredible too. And I want to see you embrace your incredible."

I huffed out a quick guffaw. "I do too."

"Then trust me to help you. We'll start slow. Maybe hum some songs and see what comes of it. If you want to sing, great. If not, there's always tomorrow, yeah?"

At his encouragement, I nodded my agreement. His hands left my face to slide into my ponytail and down my back. My hair sprang loose as he pulled the tie down, spreading my hair and running his fingers through it.

"I've been wondering what you look like with your hair down. The ponytail is for your students. The way you look with your hair down, your eyes soft, skin flushed...that look is just for me and our music together."

My hippie lifeguard was a romantic.

If I wasn't already seated, I would have lost all control over my legs at that statement and that heated stare he was giving me. My cheeks burned hotter and I knew right then I'd made the right choice by being honest with him.

He sat back down and placed the ukulele on his lap again. "I know it seems cliché for me to play the ukulele, but it reminds me of home. We used to sit around the house, the backyard, the beach, around campfires. Really, anywhere people were gathered, someone would break out an ukulele and the singing would start. It didn't matter what your voice sounded like, or how well you played. It was about being together and sharing reminders of your ancestry, your culture."

I smiled, listening to him share something so personal. I could see now where he was coming from about keeping things casual. I was so worried about singing in front of people and he'd grown up with the opposite. Everyone sang and no one thought anything of it.

"Tell me how you grew up, Hessa." Kai strummed a few chords before easing into a melody I knew I'd heard before but couldn't place.

I looked away, taking in the last of the orange and yellow streaks across the sky. Darkness was setting in, creating an intimate cocoon around us. The only source of light penetrating our bubble was the lamps on the pier in the distance. It felt as if we were the only two people left in the world, urging me to open up and share, whereas harsh daytime would have left me too exposed.

"My parents divorced when I was really little. My dad left in his RV and traveled the country making money on odd jobs wherever he happened to be. My mom tried her best, but wasn't really around much between work and boyfriends. I was always a total book nerd. I could spend all day and night in my room reading, escaping through the worlds described in the books I read. My twin sister and I were really close up until high school. I buckled down harder to get good grades and hopefully a college scholarship. She started hanging out with the wrong crowd and barely graduated. I surrounded myself with people like me at college: it was all about academics. Focused on schooling and learning. There was no time for creativity or art or music. I tried to bury that side of me since it just wasn't practical." I broke off, realizing I'd said more to Kai about my childhood than I had to anyone else.

He switched to another song, this one softer and mellower. "Then how did you find yourself writing songs?"

"I guess I had a lot of anger about my dad leaving and not caring about my sister and I. Then my sister and I had a falling out. I had all this emotion choking me and I didn't know what to do with it. So, I sat down and started writing one day. And the style I seemed to write in the most lent itself to song lyrics. I saw a keyboard for sale one day in my neighborhood as I was driving by. I swerved over to the curb, jumped out and bought it before I could think too much about it. I played around with melodies, using YouTube to teach me how to play. I don't know. I just got so much enjoyment from it, I kept doing it." I shrugged, realizing I'd never made a conscious decision to write songs. It just came naturally to me and I let myself follow my passion. Maybe for the first time in my life.

Kai was looking at me like I was a puzzle, one he very much wanted to figure out. "You say you're so practical and academic, but you're not a math or science teacher. You teach English and writing. And the way I see it, writing is entirely subjective. It can be wildly passionate, it can be dark and seductive, it can be light and irreverent." He winked at me, changing the tune on the instrument. "I would guess you're a highly passionate person,

Hessa. You just don't recognize it because you've mislabeled your-self for so long."

His words left my mind swirling, my heart feeling exposed to harsh elements. I'd never had someone challenge me like that before, or even suggest that I was more than the scholar I always claimed to be. I was proud of that label.

But it never felt like a cage before.

"I always thought it was a self-confidence issue that kept me from pursuing my music in a more public way." I tilted my head, staring at the waves reaching the shore as I sorted out what I was feeling. "Perhaps it's more to do with realizing who I really am. All the many sides to me. What I feel I can be." I looked over at Kai, wondering what he thought of all this introspection.

He had a slight smile on his face, nodding along thoughtfully. "Sounds like you have things to think about. Many questions to ask yourself. I think we all do. Or at least we all *should* from time to time. You know, check in and see if we're living the life we desire. It takes courage to ask yourself those hard questions."

He strummed one last note, then sat forward, a huge smile taking over his face. "I've got the perfect song for you. I bet you've heard it. It's been sung by a very famous Hawaiian and you hear it all the time: "Over the Rainbow." Will you sing it with me?"

I smiled back, the happiness he exuded contagious. "I'll do my best. I don't know all the words, but I'll hum what I don't know."

He winked and started plucking out the melody. I took a deep breath, threw caution to the wind and sang softly, his strong voice blending with mine. I kept going when he nodded and winked at me, like a pat on the back for finally having the courage. My voice got stronger as I felt more at ease realizing I'd survive this experi-ence. When we got to the line "...and the dreams that you've dreamed of, dreams really do come true..." my voice almost broke, the realization of why he'd chosen this song washing over me.

Writing songs was a dream of mine. One I'd buried deep. I'd convinced myself it was a pipe dream, a silly aspiration, something to keep secret while focusing on more 'important' endeavors. But my romantic heart never let the dream go.

And Kai was the first to see beyond my carefully crafted verbivore exterior to the sensual, passionate woman underneath.

I didn't know how it was possible, but as our voices wrapped around each other in the night air, so did my heart intertwine with his. I didn't expect it to happen, nor did I particularly want it to happen, but happen it did.

When the last note of "Over the Rainbow" faded under the crash of the waves, Kai and I sat in comfortable silence. I felt lighter than I had in recent years, knowing I'd faced a fear and sang in public. Yes, it was only in front of one person and it wasn't any of the songs I'd written, but it was a step. At least I'd started taking the baby steps necessary to fulfill my dream.

Finally, Kai put the ukulele back in his case, stood up and offered me his hand. This time, when I placed my hand in his, he pulled me up with enough force to launch me into his body. I landed against his hard chest, his arms coming around me, holding me there.

My eyes widened and flashed alarm at the sudden proximity. My almost drowsy state of calm from the waves and the sing-along disappeared in an instant, reminding me, like stepping into a bathtub of scalding water, I was in the presence of a hot-blooded male. One I was highly attracted to. One who made my insides flare with desire then melt into longing, knowing he was not only out of my league, but also not the type of man I was looking to get involved with.

But that wouldn't stop me from enjoying his friendship, or being pressed up against his human wall of muscle.

His hands ran up my back, tangled in my hair and pulled. My head tilted back and he took advantage, lowering his face till he was mere inches from making contact. I barely breathed, trying not to startle him out of his intention, which I was hoping included kissing me. Only half of his face was illuminated by the lights from the pier, but that one half showed me his gaze was on my lips.

"Your voice is as beautiful as you. Thank you for trusting me," he whispered. Then his face lowered even more. I closed my eyes, praying he wasn't teasing me with the slow-mo approach.

His breath gently blew across my lips before I felt his lips brush across mine, lightly at first. Then they came back, more forceful, as if the first taste wasn't nearly enough. They plucked at my lower lip, paying it specific attention. Teeth nipped, followed by his tongue soothing the quick flash of pleasure-pain. My lips parted, so intrigued by this divide-and-conquer assault they tried to let a gasp through. The flash of his tongue sliding in, tasting, tempting, titillating, swept away all thoughts of technique or alliteration.

All that was left was sensation: the hard tug on my hair, the goose bumps covering every square inch of skin, the chills racing up and down my spine, the heartbeat racing out of control, the heat centering in my core.

I never wanted it to stop.

Out of control and finally out of my head, I used my hands to grab handfuls of his polo shirt, pulling him closer, then releasing to explore the exposed skin. My arms wrapped around his back, then searched lower, finding twin globes of hard muscle. That too, I wanted closer. Pulling him into me, I found the booty in more ways than one. Yes, I had my hands on that fantastic backside of his, but it also pressed him into me, the ultimate treasure found in the form of his hard length against my belly.

Either that or he carried a steel pipe in his shorts.

Kai broke off the kiss, his hands still fisted in my hair. He was breathing hard and his jaw was clenched. My mind just screamed one word on repeat: no, no, no. I wanted his lips back. I was already addicted and would shamelessly beg if necessary. You can't give a girl a glimpse of paradise and then snatch it away.

Like stealing candy from a baby, or chocolate from a fat girl. It just wasn't done. At least not without an ugly tantrum.

"Ono..." Kai groaned the word, then kissed my forehead, released my hair and set me away from him. "Let's get you back to your car, yeah?"

The chill from the night air, the sudden loss of Kai's warmth and my own self-doubt kicked in, leaving me adrift without a clue what all just happened tonight.

After tossing and turning, followed by disturbing dreams of heaven and hell, I finally woke the next morning to my alarm blaring. I stepped into the bathroom to get ready for work. One glimpse in the mirror and I could have sworn my lips still looked swollen. Or at least changed, so momentous was the kiss from last night. Would my coworkers be able to tell? Would my students know I was one step closer to actually completing my mystery dare of singing in front of a public group?

I turned on my phone and found the song I was looking for: Just a Kiss by Lady Antebellum. I hit repeat and lost myself in the haunting words. I replayed everything from last night: the conversation, the looks, the music. The Kiss. Yep, it was getting capital letters now.

Before I could get ahead of myself and try to second-guess what Kai was feeling or what he wanted from me, I needed to focus first on what I wanted. Was I even interested in getting into a relationship with him? I knew I was attracted to him something fierce, but did I want more?

I'd spent way too many years hating my fickle father for leaving my sister and I when we needed another parent. Who just takes off and forgets about their kids? I knew he loved us in his own way, but having the freedom to travel as he pleased came before being a parent, which was totally wrong.

Kai seemed more responsible than that, but he did have a lot of the same tendencies. He went barefoot everywhere, he talked about spending time outside in nature being essential to living. He meditated, for God's sake! My father thought he could make a domesticated type of life work too when he married my mom. He only lasted a few years before he ran out of there, escaping the suburbia doldrums for more a more exciting life on the road.

Bottom-line, I didn't know Kai well enough to guess as to what he wanted or what he'd do in life. I'd have to get to know him better and until then, reign in my emotions so I didn't get caught up in what his kisses did to my body.

With my new intentions set, I paused the music, shoved my graded papers in my giant handbag and I was out the door to teach some reading and writing to my high schoolers. As I opened the front door, I nearly tripped, my bag flying and landing on the cement pathway leading to my driveway. I was about to chuckle, thinking I'd lucked out by not having hot coffee in my hands this morning, when my eyes took in what was beyond my bag, the chuckle dying a sad little death.

My front lawn looked like a political campaign puked all over my grass. At least two dozen wood stakes were piercing my lawn, with bright yellow posters attached to the top. Each sign had my name written in black ink at the top, followed by one simple sentence: *You've Been Dared...Now Do It.*

A neighbor, driving by on his way to work, slowed down to read the signs, then honked and waived at me before taking off. Like this was all some joke. Or some weird prank one of my friends pulled on me, like an adult version of TP'ing.

But this wasn't a joke or a prank. This was my life, my secret, being exposed to neighbors and friends. This was my privacy going up in smoke.

9

ai

I barely slept last night, tossing and turning over the image of Hessa on the beach, backlit by the pier, opening up to me about her past. I had kept my hands busy on my ukulele not because I wanted to play it so badly, but because I had to stop myself from reaching out and pulling her onto my lap.

Taking her hair down was a big mistake. It made me think of lazy Sunday mornings, waking up to find her asleep next to me, hair spread out over my pillow. It was a private, unrestrained side of her no one else was allowed to see.

And that was all before she'd opened her mouth to sing with me. As touristy as the song had become, there was something about "Over the Rainbow" that made my heart ache for my island home. To hear Hessa's voice mixed with mine, singing a song that spoke to me on such a heart level was something I couldn't describe.

I was honored that she'd opened up to me and allowed me to

hear her singing voice. I knew that was a big step for her, one I didn't take for granted.

Now I just needed to see her again to make sure she didn't slip back into the snooty schoolteacher. There was no question I wanted to spend more time with her. Question was, would Hessa want to spend time with a hippy lifeguard far from home? I wasn't intellectual at all, yet that seemed like something she held in high regard.

I was headed into work early to see if I could pull some extra shifts the next few weeks. Usually Ivan would accommodate if he had the slots to give. I was hoping to accrue some extra cash to dump into my old VW van. I felt like it was time to finally clean her up and get her in better shape.

I refused to delve too deep into my change of heart on her condition. I couldn't wait to get a certain school teacher into my VW and take her on a quick road trip up the coast. But that wasn't going to happen in her current state. Hessa deserved better than that.

My phone rang from the cupholder. I glanced quickly at the screen, surprised and quite pleased to see Hessa's name pop up. "Good morning, Sunshine."

"Oh...uh, good morning. I-I seem to have a problem." Hessa's voice sounded worried and distracted. Something was wrong.

"What's going on?"

I could hear her breath huffing into the phone, interspersed with a clunking sound. "I came out of my house this morning to find stakes all over my front lawn with signs egging me on to do my dare. I'm removing them so I'm not the laughing stock of my neighborhood."

Anger on her behalf flooded my brain. I tightened my hands on the wheel, choosing not to do my meditation breaths like usual. I was pissed and I wanted that anger to fuel my search for the asshole who did this to her. Someone had come onto her property and vandalized it over this stupid dare.

"You don't happen to have security cameras, do you?" I'd known something was up two weeks ago and hadn't pushed hard enough. We had to catch whoever was doing this and shut them down before anything worse happened. The fact that they were targeting Hessa at her home was chilling.

"No, I don't have cameras! I don't even lock my backdoor half the time!" Hessa's voice wobbled, cluing me into her fragile state.

I realized she was on the edge of losing it completely. I needed to calm down and comfort her first. Finding the guy could come later.

"No problem. Can you take a picture real quick of your yard?" I spoke calmly, hoping she'd let me help her.

She took a deep breath. "I did. Right before I called you."

"Okay, that's great. I'm glad you thought to do that. How about I come by and help you out? What's your address?"

"You don't need to come over. I can get the rest and still make it to school on time." Hessa already had her emotions in check and didn't need anyone's help.

"I know you can, but I'd like to help anyway. What's your address?"

She sighed. "7216 Southwind Circle, west of Beach."

"I know where that is. I'm pretty close, can be there in two minutes. How about you stay on the phone with me till I get there?"

"Okay."

There was a long pause. I didn't hear her pulling up stakes so I took the moment to say what I had been planning to say to her when I called her later. "Thank you for last night. Best night I've had in a long time. Want to do it again, this time you try the ukulele?"

She huffed out a laugh. "I'll try, but I only know how to play a few chords on the guitar, and even that's just what I've taught myself."

"Nah, I'll teach you. Then you can teach me one of your songs.

Deal?" I cringed, crossing my fingers mentally while I waited for her answer.

"Hmm...maybe. We'll see."

Before I could press for a firmer answer, I pulled up to her house to see her prim and proper in her schoolteacher outfit, yard a mess of signs and dirt all around her. I jumped out of my truck, came around the back and pulled her into my arms. I tucked her head under my chin, enjoying her soft warmth pressed against me. My hand moved up and down her back while I whispered nonsensical soothing things in her ear.

After a few moments, she tilted her head back to give me a watery smile. I pushed her glasses back up her nose and kissed her quickly, hating the tears in her eyes, but loving that she trusted me to be there for her. "Why don't you go get another cup of coffee while I clean the rest of this up, okay?"

"Okay," she whispered. "Thank you."

I watched her walk back up to her front door, that skirt and those heels too much to turn away from just yet. She turned back around in the doorway to catch me leering at her. I gave her a wink, enjoying the way her cheeks burned in reaction. She rolled her eyes and went into the house, robbing me of my eye candy.

It only took me ten more minutes to clean up her yard and tamp down the patches of grass that had been disrupted. I also texted Jack, letting him know what happened. He texted back that if Hessa wanted to press charges later down the road, he'd get a squad car out there later to document it. I'd have to ask her. I wasn't sure what she'd want to do. I wanted her to nail the guy, but she might not feel the same.

She came back out with a coffee for me in a metal to-go cup that said 'Spell check yourself before you wreck yourself'. The nerd was alive and well in this one...and I freaking loved it. I walked her to her car, after making sure she locked her front door. A crazy guy was out there with a vendetta against her for some reason and he knew her home address. Not a good idea to leave things unlocked from now on.

I gave her another quick kiss, then watched her drive off to work. There was something crazy domestic about the situation that both shocked me and yet it seemed so right. I realized with a pang in my heart, I wanted this scenario every morning. I wanted to kiss her hello and goodbye, comfort her when she was over-whelmed, have her send me off to work with coffee in her silly mugs.

I drove off knowing I'd fallen deeper into this desire for a rela-tionship with Hessa, and I still didn't have any idea if that's what she wanted too.

Hessa

I left school on Friday, ecstatic for the weekend. The week had been a draining mix of highs and lows. My kiss with Kai was defi-nitely the high. The vandalism was the low, but even that came with a high when Kai showed up to help me. And to dole out more of those kisses.

Now I was off to meet the Squad at Strike Ready, Brinley and Shasta's self-defense studio. The girls had caught wind of what happened to my yard and they insisted I learn some moves to defend myself if it came down to it. I thought they were being overly dramatic, but could also kind of see their point. It wouldn't hurt to be a little more aware of my surroundings in general. Plus, it would be fun to hang with the Squad again...as long as Bailey didn't hound me like last time.

"Yo, yo, yo! Come on in, Hessa," Shasta yelled over at me as I entered the door to her studio. The girls were all sitting in a circle on the mats, stretching.

"Am I late?" I hated being late, which meant I obsessed about being five to ten minutes early to everything. I hustled over, had a seat, and started to stretch, not wanting to hold them up.

"No, you're right on time. I've just started setting all of Bailey's clocks ahead by fifteen minutes. That way she's not chronically late anymore," Esa piped up.

Bailey gasped. "That is so wrong, bitch. I was fashionably late. Now I'm the annoying early one. No offense, Hessa." Bailey glared at Esa, barely glancing at me with her flippant semi-apology.

"Oh sure, no offense taken. Even though you've clearly said something offensive. What's the point of saying 'no offense' all the time, when it's clearly offensive?" Brinley said to Bailey, now crossing her arms, glaring at her. I was finding Brinley to be a stickler about being kind to people. I was happy she was defending me, but I didn't think sticking it to Bailey was a good thing. It was like poking a sleeping bear.

Bailey looked taken aback, like she hadn't thought of it that way. "I guess I just say that phrase when I speak my opinion but I don't want someone to take it personally. I happen to abhor showing up on time, especially early. That's just me. Maybe someone like Hessa here doesn't mind it. Hence, my 'no offense'. See? It even rhymes. I was trying to be kind, so get off my ass, BB."

Oh crappers, Bailey was getting wound up again. At this rate, we'd never get to the self-defense stuff.

"Ladies!" Esa jumped up, cutting off any further snarky responses. "We're here to help our girl, Hessa. Not to bitch at each other, like chimps fighting over the last banana. So zip it and let Shasta talk, okay?"

I shook my head slowly, eyes wide. Chimps? This was getting crazier than that student I had a few years ago that wanted to dare her partner to flash a crowd of clowns, Mardi Gras style. Nothing about it made sense, but it was funnier than hell if you didn't think about it too much.

Shasta stood up. "Thank you, Esa." Then she looked at all of us, a big smile on her face. She launched into a description of the moves we were going to learn that day, like the girl's spat was an everyday occurrence. Part of me was appalled. The other part of me liked that I had a group of women surrounding me that told it like it was, rather than sugar-coating everything. Plus, they were all here today to support me. A girl could search all her life for that kind of female friendship.

We paired up and moved through some basic drills to warm up, then practiced some hand grab maneuvers. We finished up with choke escapes, both standing and laying down.

I didn't have a brother growing up, nor had I been involved in sports, so the full body contact was awkward and uncomfortable at first. But when someone puts their hands on your neck with the intent to strangle you, you get over your discomfort expediently. Survival instincts kicked in and I began to enjoy the physical nature of rolling someone off of me. It made me feel strong, capable, in charge of my own body.

Shasta called it a day when we were all wiping sweat off our foreheads, arms and necks bright red from our movements. We agreed to walk over to Chocolate Dreams and have a reward for our hard work in the form of decadent hot chocolates.

After we settled into a table and got our lips on that first sip of heaven, Bailey blurted out a question, directed at me. "So what's up with you and Kai, Hessa-girl?"

I just about spit out my chocolate. "Wh-what do you mean?"

"Well, I heard you've gone on a few dates. So, what's the scoop? You into him?" All the other ladies leaned in, intent on catching every word of this conversation.

I set my chocolate cup down on the table and pulled my hair back into a smoother ponytail without the flyaways, needing the extra time to collect my thoughts. I had nothing to hide, but I wasn't even sure what was going on yet, so how could I tell them?

"Interesting....stall tactics." Brinley's face lit up in a wicked smile directed at the girls. Then she turned to me with a wink and an explanation. "I know all about that. They questioned me hard core when I started dating Dean. You might as well just spill it before they pull it out of you. They won't stop. Resistance is futile."

They all burst out laughing, heads nodding, confirming their resolve to know about my involvement with Kai.

I rolled my eyes, reverting to teenage behavior, since this entire conversation felt very similar to other ones I'd had at that age. "Okay, all right already. Yes, I've been out with Kai a few times recently, though I wouldn't go so far as to call them official dates. We've just been meeting up at the beach."

"Wait, why wouldn't you call them dates?" Shasta's face was screwed up in confusion.

"Well, we met up to talk about the Care Dare situation. It just happened to be on the beach. And then he asked me to meet him again. Totally not a date." I hadn't really classified it like that in my own head, so saying it out loud deflated the happy bubble I'd been living in the last few days. Maybe I really was reading too much into it.

"Hmm...I don't know. Sounds like a date to me. Dean told me he saw you guys sitting on the sand, and not like a friend distance away. More like practically sitting on each other's lap." Brinley had a sly grin on her face.

"Was Dean spying on us?" I didn't like the idea of anyone I knew watching us. That time together felt so private, it was weird to think Dean saw us.

"No, of course not! But it *is* a public beach, you know?" Brinley frowned, not liking my insinuation.

I shook my head, not meeting her eyes. "Sorry, that didn't come out right. I know he wouldn't spy. It just felt weird knowing someone had seen us." I sighed. "I don't know what to call our meetings. They felt like dates, but we didn't really talk about the significance or what we are to each other."

"Sooooo...?" Esa had a smile on her face, motioning with her hands for me to continue.

"So...what?"

"Did you kiss or hug or even just touch in a super friendly way?" Esa asked.

"Smoldering glances?" Bailey added.

"Sexy flirting?" Shasta interjected.

"All of the above...?" I answered like it was a question, but technically, our 'meetings' did have all of the above.

There was a moment's pause while they processed what I meant. Then all four girls exploded with whoops and hollers. Brinley reached over the table to high-five me.

"Thatta girl, Hessa," Bailey encouraged me.

I threw back my head and laughed. These girls were crazy and I loved them.

"I guess we'll call them dates?" I looked around the table at their faces, knowing their answers already.

"Hell yeah, we will!" Esa shouted. Then she settled down a bit. "Now the question is what do you want to do from here. Do you like him? Do you want to go on more dates? What's your next move?"

"Whoa, hold up, lady. We're not all trying to get married like you. I'm planning to just enjoy the time I get with him and see what happens." I went back to sipping my hot chocolate, content in my plan.

"What?" Shasta had her face all screwed up again. "That's your plan?? Just see what happens? That's a shit plan, excuse my French. You gotta take the bull by the horns. This is not the 1800's anymore. You gotta woman-up and go for what you want."

"Yeehaw! Shasta is on a roll!" Brinley cracked up laughing.

"She's got a point though. You gotta go for what you want. Do you want Kai?" Esa was smiling at me, ever the peacemaker.

And wasn't that the ultimate question. I wasn't sure if I just wanted him for something temporary and nice, or if I wanted him for something more. And I'm pretty sure the decent thing would be to figure that out before things went any further between us.

"I'm definitely attracted to him. I just don't know if he's right for me or not. That's why I'm taking the 'wait and see' approach. But I promise you, if or when I decide he's what I want, I will go after him with every ounce of my energy. And you'll know about it, because I'll be coming to you for advice. Sound good?" I didn't need their approval, but I did want it.

"That's reasonable. I dig it." Brinley smiled at me, then looked around the table. Everyone else gave me a thumbs-up, so I took that as their stamp of approval.

We sat in companionable silence, finishing our hot chocolates. I may have had a crazy person targeting me, but I felt pretty damn good. I had a hottie lifeguard looking out for me, self-defense lessons under my belt, and a crew of crazy-ass girlfriends who'd call me on my shit but also protect me no matter what. The addition of these women to my life seemed like total serendipity.

"I'm sorry. Am I the only here who wants to back up and talk about the kissing?" Bailey looked at us, a serious expression on her face.

"Jeepers...."

Did I mention how crazy my Beach Squad was?

Hessa

My house phone rang just a few minutes past five o'clock Saturday morning. It jerked me out of a deep sleep, frightening me with what it could mean. No one knew that number. And certainly no marketer was going to be calling that early on a weekend. Not one that didn't want a lawsuit from a hungry lawyer and a sleep-deprived, angry client.

I rolled out of bed, fumbled for my glasses and answered the phone in the bedroom next to mine that I'd designated as a home office.

"Hessa? This is Mr. Brown." My principal's gravely voice came through the phone.

This couldn't be good. I sat down hard in the desk chair, clearing my throat and the cobwebs from a deep sleep before speaking.

"What's going on?"

"We just got a call from the police. They need you and I to come down to the police station and have a chat with them about one of our students, Gabe Martinez."

I flipped through the names of my students in my head. Gabe was in my third period English class, friends with James, if I recalled correctly. He didn't do Jr. Lifeguards with James though this last summer like they usually did. In fact, he'd been getting into more and more trouble lately. If the police were involved, it must be pretty serious.

"Sure. I can be there in thirty minutes. May I ask why they want to speak to me?" I wasn't sure what help I could be. I didn't recall hearing him talk about anything particularly dangerous.

"He was attempting a Care Dare late last night when he wound up in the hospital." Mr. Brown's voice was quiet but his words echoed through my mind the whole time I rushed to get ready.

essa

The hospital smell hit me like a wall when the automatic doors swooshed open. Mr. Brown was a silent statue next to me, his only communication a stiff head nod when I met him in the chilly hospital parking lot. My stomach was tied in knots. I hadn't even remembered to bring my stack of Care Dare submissions with me to try to piece together what may have happened.

I was confused about the whole thing since I hadn't assigned any approved dares yet.

I was scared for my student.

I was worried about the integrity of the whole Care Dare program.

Hallway after hallway blended together until we were finally at a nurse's station. Mr. Brown asked for Gabe Martinez' room number. The nurse led us down another long hallway before stopping outside a closed door. She told us to wait there while she went in and talked to Gabe's parents.

I tapped my leg while we waited, unable to control the tick. My anxiety rose the longer she was in there and the tighter Mr. Brown clenched his jaw.

The door finally opened and I thought I would pass out from holding my breath.

"You can go on in now. The patient's mother is in the room and expecting you." The nurse gave us a tired smile and moved back down the hallway from where we'd come.

Mr. Brown held the door open and swept his hand, indicating I should go first. I threw my shoulders back, smoothed my face and walked in the room. The beeping of machines greeted me a split second before the hate-filled scowl on the woman's face. She was sitting in a chair next to the bed, holding Gabe's hand. His eyes were closed and there was a white bandage wrapped around his head.

I waited till Mr. Brown was standing next to me. I paused to let him take the lead. When he didn't say anything, I stepped forward and extended my hand to Gabe's mother.

I whispered, trying not to disturb Gabe. "Hello, Ms. Martinez. I'm Hessa Woodland, Gabe's English teacher. I'm so sorry to meet you this way."

Her eyes lowered to my outstretched hand before snapping back to my face, eyes ablaze. "You're the one daring my son to jump his motorcycle? What were you thinking?"

I visibly pulled back, I was so surprised at her accusation. "I-I'm sorry?"

"You should be. Look at him!" She tilted her head in Gabe's direction. "He's in a medically induced coma. He has a concussion and they want to make sure the swelling goes down before waking him up."

I shook my head, my eyes focused on Gabe. Tears blurred my vision seeing him motionless like that. I couldn't look away, even when Mr. Brown finally spoke up.

"Ms. Martinez, I'm sorry to see your son in this condition. I truly am. However, I think we need to investigate what happened before we place blame." His forehead was dotted with beads of sweat, though the temperature was bordering on glacial in the room.

"I have his phone. His last text was to his best friend, James. He said he had to do this dare or he'd never hear the end of it. What else could he have meant?" Ms. Martinez was back to glaring at me, skewering me with her eyes.

The tips of my ears burned under her accusation. I willed myself not to cry in front of her, even though it felt like an elephant was sitting on my chest. I loved my students, no matter how irritated they made me on a day-to-day basis. I couldn't imagine how scared she must be right now, seeing her son lying in a hospital bed. The shame of her accusation was making my head pound, even though I was thoroughly confused as to how this could actually be my fault.

I dragged my eyes away from Gabe and focused on his mother. "Ms. Martinez. I absolutely hate to see this happen to Gabe. I'll do whatever I can to find out what happened last night. We'll make this right, you'll see." I nodded my head, vowing to myself that no matter what, I'd see this thing through and make it right for him and his family. I believed whole-heartedly that the Care Dare program had nothing to do with it, but I'd prove it to her and still make sure she and Gabe got the support they needed.

Mr. Brown jumped in, pulling at his collar. "Let's let the officials investigate and then we'll talk about what can be done here. Ms. Martinez, my best wishes for your son's speedy recovery."

With that, he grabbed my arm and practically dragged me out of the room. He didn't let go of my arm until we hit the lobby, making me feel like a reprimanded little child. I didn't know what his problem was, but he'd better think thrice before touching me again like that.

When the doors opened up, spilling us into the fresh air of

the parking lot, I whipped around, ready to confront his man-handling. I opened my mouth, but the words were cut off before they even started when he raised his hand in front of my face.

"I don't want to hear it." His face was ashen but there was fire in his eyes as he stared me down. "You need to not say anything to anyone. Do you hear me?"

I shook my head, not understanding what he was talking about.

He sighed, seeming exasperated with me. "Until we get our lawyers in here and the police determine what happened, you can't say a word to anyone, especially Ms. Martinez. You express anything that can be construed as guilt or responsibility and the district will be facing a lawsuit."

The confusion left quickly as I realized all he cared about was a damn lawsuit. "Mr. Brown, her son is laying in a coma right now." I was so furious. "Our focus should be on helping our student, not worrying about what the lawyers will say."

He took another small step toward me, invading my personal space. He dropped his voice and made his position clear. "You say one word, to anyone, I will have to fire you. I don't want to Hessa. You're an excellent teacher. But I won't allow this incident to ruin our school's reputation or our financial standing. Am I clear?"

I almost couldn't get words out, my throat was so clogged. "Crystal," I said through clenched teeth. I whirled around and practically ran to my car. Tears were threatening to spill over and I wouldn't allow him to see that he'd gotten to me. I hated this reaction. When I was this angry, the emotion came out in the form of tears, not the harsh put-down I wished for.

I fumbled for my keys, practically ripping the door off my poor car and heaving myself inside. I knew I needed to calm down before I drove anywhere, so I dropped my head to the steering wheel and took deep breaths, willing my heart rate to slow down.

Seeing Gabe so motionless in that stark white hospital bed

made him seem so young and innocent. I was horrified that he was in that condition. I was worried about his prognosis. I was confused as to how the Care Dare program could have been responsible. I was furious at the principal for showing his true colors by only caring about lawyers and lawsuits instead of the children we were charged with caring for. I felt so alone in shouldering the responsibility of one of my students. I let the tears fall, letting myself feel all the raging emotions swirling in my body.

When the storm dissipated, only one thing sounded right.

I lifted my head, wiped my cheeks, and picked up my cell phone. I hit Kai's number and prayed he'd pick up.

"Hessa?"

"Kai." I only got out the one word. I wasn't sure where to start and I knew I couldn't trust my voice yet.

"What's wrong? Are you okay?" Kai's voice immediately took on an urgent tone. I could hear noise in the background but couldn't make out where he might be or if he had time for me.

"Sorry. Yes, I'm doing okay. Is now a good time?" Maybe I shouldn't have called. Maybe I should have gone home first and sorted out any documentation about Gabe's Care Dare.

"Of course I have time for you. And if I was busy, I'd make time. I'll ask again: what's going on?" Kai said it so matter-of-fact, like it was obvious he had time for me. Maybe there was more to that kiss the other night than I originally thought.

I shook my head, forcing myself to stay focused on Gabe. I didn't have time to dissect kisses or relationship statuses. "I just visited one of my students in the hospital. His mom said he was dared to jump his motorcycle over a car last night and he didn't clear it. My principal threatened me not to talk about it because of a potential lawsuit, but you should have seen him, Kai. He was so small lying there in that bed! I have to figure out what happened. I have to help his mom. There'll be hospital bills and I'm sure his motorcycle is trashed. And that's just if he pulls out of the coma okay! What if he doesn't? Or if he does and he has impaired brain function!"

"Hessa!" Kai barked into the phone cutting me off, which was just as well. I felt the hysteria climbing back up my throat. I dropped my forehead to the steering wheel again, phone pressed tightly to my ear, and focused on taking deep breaths.

"Ono, you have to stay calm. Let's talk about this and sort everything out, okay? Where are you?" Kai spoke softly, the smooth cadence of his voice doing more to calm me than the meditation breaths I was still working on.

"I'm in my car in the hospital parking lot off Beach Blvd."

"Are you okay to drive?" Kai seemed doubtful.

"Certainly." I just had to remember to breath.

"Listen, I'm at work covering someone's shift. I don't get off till noon. Why don't you go home, collect your thoughts and any communication you may have had with Gabe about the dare, and I'll come meet you when I'm off?"

"That would be great. Thank you." I was grateful he was willing to talk it out with me. Just having someone else to talk to about the whole thing sounded heavenly. Like the burden was too much to bear with just one person.

"Anytime. I'm sorry I can't be there earlier. Text me when you get safely to your house."

Gah, the guy was so sweet. My lips lifted, the hint of a smile coming out despite the cry-fest puffy eyes.

"I will. Talk soon." I hung up the phone and shifted into gear, carefully making my way home.

Kai

"The kid said it was a dare. That can't be a coincident, right?" I was on the phone with Jack, having called him the minute I hung up with Hessa. The pit in my stomach was intensifying with each person that was put in the hospital.

"No way to tell quite yet, but my gut says no, that's no coincidence. Let me put more pressure on my IT guy and see if he can come up with anything." Jack seemed stressed, as usual.

"Can you swing by Hessa's place tonight and talk to her? Or at least go talk to Gabe's mom at the hospital?" I cared about the kid's well-being, but my first priority was making sure we had evidence that cleared Hessa of any wrong doing. I didn't think her Care Dare program was a good idea, but I also would bet my VW that her program had nothing to do with these dangerous dares going around.

"Another detective already talked to Ms. Martinez last night and again this morning. I'll talk with him and see if our two cases are linked. If I find anything I'll swing by Hessa's. You planning to be there?"

"For as long as she'll have me, yeah." I gripped the phone tighter, determined to get Hessa to agree to let me stay with her.

Jack chuckled. "So that's how it is, huh?"

"Damn right it is."

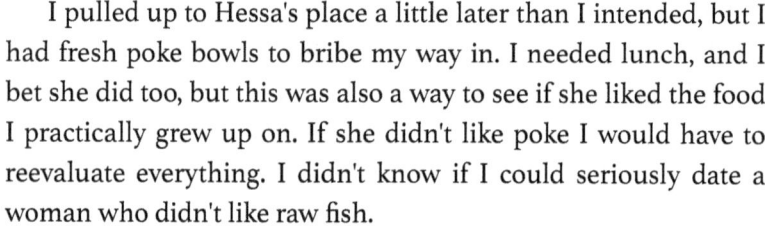

I pulled up to Hessa's place a little later than I intended, but I had fresh poke bowls to bribe my way in. I needed lunch, and I bet she did too, but this was also a way to see if she liked the food I practically grew up on. If she didn't like poke I would have to reevaluate everything. I didn't know if I could seriously date a woman who didn't like raw fish.

I was kidding.

Kind of.

Hessa swung open the front door and let me pass. She shut the door behind me and indicated I could take the bags into the kitchen, but I was too busy eying her outfit choice to keep walking. I'd seen prim and proper Ms. Woodland who I liked very, very much. I'd seen the hair down, singing on the beach in the moonlight Hessa and I liked her equally as well. Now I was laying my eyes on casual, no facades Hessa.

Her hair was pulled into a messy bun on top of her head with her glasses crookedly jammed in there. Her eyes were puffy and red from crying, I presumed. Short shorts highlighted her sexy legs, followed by a tight tank top that barely contained her breasts. My eyes drifted down and took in her feet, turning me on with the sight of her bright red toenails against her pale skin. I bet she didn't show many people this casual side of her and I was flattered that she'd shown me.

She cleared her throat and when my eyes came back up to her face, I saw that she had an eyebrow lifted, clearly catching me checking her out.

Can't blame a guy for looking at beauty when it was right in front of him. I smiled, shrugged my shoulders and took the take-out bags into the kitchen, hefting them onto the counter. Hessa started to open the bags, but I pulled her away and wrapped her in a hug instead. I waited till she relaxed into me, letting me feel her body pressed against mine.

"How you holding up?" I whispered to the side of her head. My hands couldn't stay still so I let them roam up and down Hessa's back, massaging away the tension I felt there.

"Well, I've stopped crying, so that's improvement." I felt her smile against my chest.

"I'm glad to hear it, but if you need to cry again, don't hold back on my account. Sometimes getting it out makes things better." I had a mom who wasn't afraid to show emotion. She'd taught me that we weren't to be afraid of emotions. Simply let them be and let them teach you.

Hessa pulled back to scan my face. "You're not afraid to see a girl cry in front of you?"

I chuckled. "No, Ono. You cry, I'll cry with you."

She slowly shook her head. "You're too sweet. I'm not sure what to say to that."

"Tell me you love poke."

"I love poke." No hesitation.

"Then all is well. Let's eat and then we'll talk, yeah?"

We grabbed our food, sat down at my tiny kitchen table, and talked all about my last few shifts, our favorite foods, the kids I had in Jr. Lifeguards that were also Hessa's students. Basically, we kept it light and purposely danced around the drama from this morning. I was enjoying seeing Hessa's smile and her occasional laugh. She was flat out gorgeous when she laughed. Her eyes would squint shut and she'd toss her head back, letting a smile take over her face. Her laugh was loud, the type you could hear throughout the whole house. It was the best sound I'd heard in a long time.

But all good things must end at some point. When I couldn't eat even one more piece of fish, I gathered up our containers, threw them in the trash and then pulled Hessa to her feet. We walked into the living room and sat down on the couch side by side. I kept her hand in my lap, stroking my thumb over the soft skin on the back of her hand.

"Tell me from the beginning." No point ignoring it any longer. I was there to help her and that meant I needed every single detail about her student.

She sighed, pulling her feet up under her on the couch and proceeded to tell me everything that had happened that morning. I tried to remain calm, but when she told me about Ms. Martinez blaming her for what happened, I had to jump in.

"You know this is not your fault, right?" I squeezed her hand tighter. She met my eyes and I saw they'd filled with tears.

I immediately pulled her onto my lap and hugged her, trying to break through her fog of guilt.

"This is not your fault, Hessa. You can feel badly for Gabe. You can want to help. But you cannot blame yourself. Do you hear me?"

"I hear you, I'm just having a hard time believing it." Her voice came out strangled from holding back the tears.

"Change your thoughts, change your beliefs. So, I want you to start saying in your head that you have sympathy for Gabe. You want the best for him. You want him to come out of this okay. You will do what you can to help him and his mom. You will only accept the part you may have played in this. You will not take on anything that isn't yours to bear. Gabe and his mother must also shoulder their part in this. Don't take that lesson away from them." I pulled her away from my chest to see if she was following me.

Her brows were pulled together and she looked like she was thinking it over.

"It may sound like some bullshit woo woo, but I promise you, your thoughts control how you feel. When my parents divorced, I felt responsible for awhile. I was acting out, not doing well in school, just angry with the world. My dad pulled me aside one day and gave me a lecture. But not the standard parent lecture you'd think. He told me that I was the only person who could change my life. That my thoughts determined my emotions and my actions. I needed to take responsibility for my own life and make it what I wanted. I don't know why it resonated that day, but it did. I couldn't control a lot of things in my life, but I could control my thoughts. So I did. And I started to build the life I wanted." I wound down, unsure if I'd completely lost her in my rambling.

Hessa

. . .

I was sitting on his lap, listening to him share about his childhood and what kind of man he was today. I didn't know if it was the full stomach or the warm hugs or the way his hazel eyes burned into mine, but it was like a tidal wave crashed into me, leaving me with only one thought.

I wanted this man.

I wanted to talk to him every day. I wanted to sing with him. I wanted to share the details of my day with him. I wanted to press my body against his warm skin every minute of every day.

Heavens to Betsy! He was a good man. To his very core. And that was flipping hot. I had to taste him. I had to get closer.

I didn't think it through. I didn't analyze a pros and cons list. I didn't weigh the consequences. I just dove in, flying blind and switching my brain off completely. My M.O. was to analyze every detail before making a logical decision about everything from the toothpaste brand I used to the people I allowed as 'friends' on Instabook. I was so far from logical at that moment, I couldn't remember what the word meant.

I grabbed the front of his white polo shirt and pulled him into me, crushing his lips under mine. For one horrifying second, he was frozen. Before I could pull away to second-guess my abrupt veer from sanity, his hands jumped into action by pulling me into his chest, my breasts squeezed between us. Lips moved over mine, pushing my mouth apart, allowing his tongue to dive in and sweep away all remaining vestiges of rational thought.

I was a mass of feelings and sensations, oblivious to the world around me. The world tilted and I reveled in the feeling, not realizing till Kai's body was pressed against mine, toes to lips, that he'd flipped me around to lay back on my couch.

One hand gripped my jaw, holding my face in place while he attacked my lips with a skill I didn't know existed. The other hand was squeezing my breast causing my back to arch in a desperate attempt to push more flesh into his grip.

I was in a Kai frenzy and I didn't care that this was completely out of character for me. I wanted more lips, more skin, more tingles running up and down my spine.

Kai broke away from my mouth, his lips trailing down to my collarbone before dropping to my shoulder and falling still. I lifted my hips, desperate for more friction, shamelessly rubbing myself against the hardness laying on me. My wanton behavior was rewarded inappropriately by his hands leaving my body. Before I could stage a proper protest, he'd pushed up off my body, sitting back down on the couch, my legs over his lap.

I lay there for a moment, forcing myself to breath and come down from the sexual high that left me more frustrated than I'd felt this morning when my boss threatened my job over something that wasn't my fault.

Which was exactly the thought I needed, like a bucket of cold water to the face. I had to figure out what to do about Gabe. My job was on the line. My student was in the hospital. My Care Dare program was on the chopping block. Shit really hit the fan this morning.

And here I was making out with Kai, the gorgeous lifeguard who was probably appalled by my conduct. One kiss on a moonlit beach did not mean he wanted to take things further. I'd practically thrown myself at him, forcing him to make out with me. I knew I was bad at the dating thing, but this was a new low for me.

My face lit up, showcasing my embarrassment for all to see. Kai finally looked back over to me and jumped up off the couch. Great, he was going to leave, disgusted by me.

Instead, he pulled me off the couch and dipped his head to get right in my face, his nose almost brushing against mine, he was so close. His jaw was clenched tight and his eyes looked like they would singe me with a single glance. I deserved whatever he had to say.

"Stop whatever you're thinking in that head of yours. You're an absolute temptress and I intend to see where that leads later on when we have all the time in the world to focus on just each other. But I can't forget what I'm here for. We have to get to the bottom of this incident and save your job first." His face transformed into a sneaky grin, designed to melt panties and inhibitions alike. "Anytime you want to attack me, please know you have my permission and encouragement to do so."

My eyes widened as he spoke, realizing he was as into that make out session as I was. Relief spread through me, not quite eradicating the butterflies left in my stomach, but at least allowing me to crawl out of the proverbial hole in the ground I'd dug when I thought he was disgusted by me.

He saw my smile, leaned in, and brushed his lips over mine right as my doorbell rang.

11

ai

Three hundred sixty-five days per year. At least ten years I've been practicing. That means I've meditated almost four thousand times in my life. Each of those meditations found absolutely necessary to harness the control necessary to pull myself off Hessa and stop before things went too far.

The woman was a siren, calling me to her dangerous shore, blinding me to everything but her and her voice. Her little moans as I kissed her. Her luscious curves that felt like heaven under my hands.

Now that she'd initiated and I knew she wanted me, all I saw was a green light. I knew she was in, which meant I could break out the full-court press and make her mine. But first, I had to stay focused and save her job. Then I could have a free conscious as I put Operation Make Hessa Mine into action.

But first, we had to deal with whoever was at her door. Lost in the feel of her body underneath mine, I forgot I'd invited Jack to swing by if he had information on the online dares.

Hessa had her hand on the doorknob, about to open it, when I glanced down and saw the state of her tank top. I slammed a hand on the door, making sure it stayed shut while I reached out and pulled the top up higher over her left breast. I liked seeing what I'd done to her clothes, and I certainly liked seeing a portion of a pink nipple peeking out to say hello, but there wasn't a chance in hell I'd let Jack get the same greeting.

Hessa's face turned bright red right before she swatted my hand away and fixed her shirt herself. I smirked, knowing she hated to feel out of control or needing anyone else to help her. She'd have to get used to it, at least from me. I wasn't going anywhere. That kiss sealed the deal for me.

Jack walked in, taking one look at Hessa's red face, askew glasses, and my smirk, before shaking his head at me. He knew exactly what was going on before he rang the doorbell. Which was fine by me. Maybe not so much by Hessa, who silently whacked my arm as we walked behind Jack to the living room. Her face was a remarkable combination of haughty and mortified. My prim and proper Ms. Woodland was back in action. I stifled a laugh, not wanting to completely piss her off.

Hessa and I sat on the couch, the same one where we'd been intimate just moments before, the cushions still warm from our bodies. Jack sat on the chair opposite us and was inordinately busy getting some papers out of a file folder on his lap. Hessa crossed her arms over her chest and slid her glasses onto her face, slipping into her teacher facade with each passing moment. I figured it was just as well. We needed to clear her of any wrong-doing, then I could strip away the pretenses and get her on her back underneath me.

Jack slid a few sheets across the coffee table. "Do recognize any of these dares as being ones in your Care Dare program?"

Hessa leaned forward and took the offered papers. Her brow

furrowed as her eyes moved down the page quickly. "No. Absolutely not. These are crazy!" She slammed the papers down on the table and proclaimed her innocence. "I promise you, these would never be dares I approved as part of our program."

Jack took the papers back, slid them into his folder, and nodded. "I was pretty sure you'd say that. Based on the dares your students have done in the past, I figured these wouldn't be approved."

Hessa let out a relieved breath. I reached over and grabbed her hand, hoping we were one step closer to having evidence to take to her principal.

"These are some dares or challenges that my computer guy has picked up floating around the inter webs in the last two weeks. They match up with some of the dares that Kai brought to my attention, and with some other incidences that a few other officers have dealt with in the southern California area. It seems to be limited to local residences, so that's a good thing. Should be easier to trace the origin on the dares." Jack pulled a stapled pile of papers out of his folder and pushed it across the table to Hessa.

"What's this?" Hessa asked when she picked it up and flipped through the first few pages.

"That is what you take your principal. Kai told me what happened with your student in the hospital today. You'll want to make sure your principal, and your school district lawyers, have those papers. I've officially opened a case, looking for whomever is organizing this online dare game. It's clear this isn't associated with your Care Dare program, which is also stated in those papers. Lastly, you'll see a highlighted entry toward the back which shows a dare going out to a GMartnz user name two days ago. The dare was to jump a motorcycle over a parked car. We're pretty sure that matches up with what happened to your student, Gabe Martinez."

Hessa gasped, flipping through to the page he referenced. "So he was dared. But not because of my program." She jumped up and went around the table. Her arms flew around Jack's neck, squeezing him in a hug he didn't seem to mind being in. Her breasts were practically in his face. I was about to jump up and break up the lovefest when Jack swiveled his head to me through the boob buffet and winked. What a bastard.

"Wow, it's getting late. It's a shame you have to go, Jack." I was breaking this up. Now.

Hessa pulled back and almost bumped right into me, not realizing I'd moved behind her, a half second away from prying her off the handsome detective. She squeaked when I put my arm around her waist, hand on her stomach, and pulled her into me.

Jack, the asshole, got up slowly, cocky smirk in place. "It's been a pleasure, Hessa. I'll be sure to swing by with more news as it comes in."

"I'm sure an email will suffice, Detective Ramirez." My clipped words were only making his smirk grow into a full-out grin. A guy could only be expected to take so much, right?

"Don't be rude, Kai." Hessa was smiling at Jack like he was the best thing she'd seen all night. "In fact, I was going to offer myself up."

"What??" Jack and I both yelped at the same time.

She looked confused at our outburst. "You know, like maybe to lure the guy out of hiding?"

Jack burst out laughing, which only added to Hessa's confusion.

"Oh, you're talking about the case?" I clarified, a tsunami of jealousy slinking into the background.

"Um, yeah, of course I'm talking about the case. Are you guys all right?"

Jack slapped me on the back, still doubled over with laughter. I just shook my head at him. I wasn't ready to simmer down and join in the fun just yet. Seeing my straight face, he straightened up and bit back his laughter. He gave me a slight nod, like bro-code for 'Got it. I'm done teasing you'.

"That might work quite well actually as it looks you're in his sights already. Let me think about how that could work safely and I'll give you a call. Sound good?" Jack asked Hessa.

We shook hands with Jack and showed him out. As soon as the door shut, I grabbed Hessa, spun her around so her back was up against the door, and kissed the hell out of her. I gave her no room to wiggle or breathe. The caveman in me needed to dominate this kiss and remind her of who she was with.

And damn it all if her little breathy moans didn't start up again. This woman was like gasoline on a fire. One kiss, one moan, and we were ready to combust.

My hands gripped her hips, knowing she couldn't miss the instant erection that pressed into her belly. Her breasts were like a cushion between us, driving me crazy with each fast breath she took. I plundered with my tongue, my lips plucking assurance from her mouth. She responded in kind, not backing down or evading my ownership. My stomach settled, jealousy leaving altogether.

I slowed the kiss, embarrassed I'd felt the need to insert myself like that. She was panting as I pressed my forehead to hers, determined to lock away the jealousy for good.

"What was that for?" Her eyes were closed, still lost in the kiss.

"Just seemed like you enjoyed Jack a little too much. Wanted to make sure you remembered how good we are together." I wouldn't lie to her, even if it made my ego cringe at the confession.

Her eyes flew open, horrified. "I did not! I mean, yes, he's good looking, but I don't feel that way about him. At all."

"I know, I'm sorry. I shouldn't have jumped to that conclusion, but I've come to find out I have a jealous streak. I won't let that happen again. Not cool at all." I shook my head at myself. I'd never reacted that way before, not even with a prior long-term girlfriend.

"Honestly? The intelligent, modern woman in me says that

display wasn't cool, but the girly side of me kinda finds it hot." She looked down, a blush staining her cheeks.

I smiled at her own confession. "How about I drop the jealousy part and we just focus on the making out part?"

She barked out a laugh. "Sure, that works for me."

Before I could resume our newly agreed upon focus, her doorbell rang again, startling us both off the door.

"You always this busy around here?"

She looked flustered as she answered, "No, never."

We heard a woman's voice yell through the thick door. "You know I can hear you out here, right? Let me in, bitches."

We looked at each other and smiled, both of us saying at the same time, "Bailey".

Hessa swung open the door to a smiling Bailey, looking as beautiful as ever. I'd only seen her a few times, but every time I saw her I was taken aback by her flamboyant beauty. Didn't mean I appreciated Hessa any less, but everyone I knew wondered why Bailey wasn't modeling, she was that gorgeous.

When I found my voice, I asked, "Did you just call me a bitch?"

She gave me the once over before responding. "Don't take it personal. I call everyone that. Even hottie lifeguards. Who am I kidding? Especially hottie lifeguards." Then she spun to Hessa and dragged her into the living room, dismissing my existence entirely.

I followed them into the living room, not about to be left out of whatever conversation Bailey had in mind. I felt like I needed to be there to support Hessa during Hurricane Bailey.

"So I heard you got dared to sing in public by some random." Bailey plopped down on the now infamous couch, relaxing back into the cushions like she planned to stay awhile.

"Yeah, that's right. Jack was actually just here about it." Hessa sat in the chair, leaving me standing behind her, hand on her shoulder.

"Jack, huh? Too bad I missed him. I could use a little eye candy."

The two girls chuckled, obviously sharing some joke that only women understood.

"Let me cut to the chase here, Hessa. I possess certain skills. A set of skills that I think can assist you." She waggled her eyebrows and I was actually afraid for Hessa and myself, and the world in general. "Has Jack made any headway in figuring out who dared you?"

"Um, no not really. He said he has his tech guy on it but so far, he hasn't pinpointed the originator to the dares." Hessa answered hesitantly, probably wondering how Bailey, a personal shopper at Nordstrom could possibly help in this situation.

Bailey turned her beady eye to me, then back to Hessa. "I can see your confusion, but let me assure you, there's more to me than this dazzling face and my impeccable fashion taste. The question is: do you want to unleash my skills?"

The smile on Bailey's face could only be described as sinister even with all its pouty-lipped beauty trying to distract. I couldn't help wondering how my sweet, innocent Hessa got to be friends with this one.

"I'm both intrigued and scared right now, to be honest. Could you be more specific with what your set of skills entails?" Hessa filled the silence, brave enough to ask what we all wanted to know.

"I can find people, not always through legal means," she stated matter-of-fact.

"Okay, cut the cloak and dagger routine, Bailey. How exactly do you find people?" I was trying to get Hessa alone so we could get back to the making out we had agreed upon. I didn't have time for this guessing game.

"Jeez, Kai. Way to suck the fun right out of this conversation. Didn't you ever see the movie Taken?" She looked at me like I was slow. She deepened her voice, making a seriously pissed off face. *"I will find you. And I will kill you."*

Hessa looked up at me, her eyes wide. "Um...."

"Okay, seriously, this has been a wasted performance on you guys." Bailey looked all kinds of put out. She jumped up and threw her hands up in the air. "I'm a damn good computer hacker, so if you'd like I'll run through a few things and see if I can find your guy. Just give me names of who's been dared and I'll work backwards."

It only took a second or two for Hessa to catch up. "That's awesome. I've always wanted to know a computer hacker!" she squealed, jumping up. "Here's the paperwork that Jack left. Maybe take a picture of it so you have the same info to work from?"

Bailey dazzled us with a brilliant smile, happy now that someone had caught on and was giving her the reaction she was hoping for. She snapped pics of the police report on her phone and hugged Hessa. "Sit tight, Hessa-girl. I'll call you with news soon." A wink in my direction and then she was sashaying to the front door.

Hessa locked the door behind her and spun around, her jaw on the floor. "She's a hacker! How cool is that?"

She was adorable. Completely floored that Bailey could be one of those stereotypical anti-social computer hackers. I was more than a little worried that we'd unleashed a crazy person who just might mess up the investigation, but I also figured that was Jack's problem.

I pulled Hessa back into the living room, pulled her glasses off her face, and wrapped my arms around her. I was done sharing her attention with others tonight. I wanted some alone time: just her and I. Thankfully, she melted right into my body, letting me know she was interested in that plan too.

Getting her mind off the dare drama was my highest concern.

I needed her out of her head, relaxed and tapping into that wild, sensual side of herself that she rarely let out.

"Will you trust me?" I whispered in her ear.

She pulled back to look at my face. "That's extremely vague and disconcerting, you know that right?" She smiled at me as she said it, so I knew she just needed some extra data in order to make a decision.

"I'd like to help you relax, so if you trust me I'd like you to have a seat on the couch. Please."

She gave me a sly look. "It was the impeccable manners that got me. Just so you know." Then she stepped over and had a seat on one end of the couch.

I shook my head. I would love, just once, to get her so crazy, she dropped the big words and polite little phrases and just moaned with pleasure. As I walked over to her speaker, I decided that was my mission tonight. I connected my phone to the speaker and put on my Hawaiian meditation playlist, a mix of classic island songs along with guitar and ukulele cover riffs.

Hessa eyed me as I moved around her room. I could feel the weight of her stare, the anticipation thickening the air as I planned my attack.

12

essa

He was just stalking around my living room, turning things on, lighting candles. Like he owned the space. I should have been irked by the intrusion, but I actually thrilled in seeing him comfortable in my personal space. I was, however, getting antsy the longer the silence continued, second-guessing what we were doing here. I was in my scuzzy clothes, hair a mess, no make-up. Heavens to Betsy, I hadn't even shaved today!

Before I could excuse myself to clean up my appearance, Kai was back at the couch, sitting on the other end. He reached down, grabbed my feet and spun me around so my feet were now laying in his lap and I was laying back against the armrest.

"Wha--"

"Shh. Just lean back and relax." He was speaking low, barely audible over the music coming from my speaker. On the first firm stroke of his thumb in my arch, my eyes fluttered shut and I acquiesced to his request. The music sounded so similar to what he played on the beach the other night, which was quickly becoming my favorite.

I didn't know where he learned to massage like that, but my feet were the happy recipients, nearly purring from the attention.

"You have sexy feet, Hessa." My eyes popped open, thinking he had to be joking with me. One look at the heat in his eyes and I knew he meant it. Before I could argue the falseness of his statement, he kept going, his voice rumbling through my chest. "I've seen these feet in sexy black heels I hope to see again, perhaps with less clothing involved. I've seen these feet walk along the beach with me, making footprints together in my favorite place. And the red polish. I like that a lot, Hessa."

Now, I'd never found feet sexy, but with each passing moment, he was convincing me there might be some element of worthiness to those things attached to the end of my legs. There was no denying the desire I saw in his face, in the way his hands rubbed and squeezed and stroked. Hey, if he liked the red polish and the black heels, I'd be sure to wear both every damn day.

When his hands traveled up my calves and massaged the back of my knees, I closed my eyes again and enjoyed the shivers running up and down my body. I worried he could feel my goose bumps on my unshaven legs, but if he did, he didn't seem put off by it in the slightest. Those hands kept stroking, higher and higher, finally hitting the hem of my shorts.

Apparently, that was no barrier either as his thumbs found their way underneath. We both gasped at the contact and his thumbs froze in place.

My eyes popped open, my head whipped up, and my cheeks turned bright red, all in the space of a nanosecond.

"No underwear, Ono?" He didn't look horrified, per say. In fact, I'd say his eyes lost all focus and the clench of his jaw matched every other muscle in his body. He looked ready to either pounce or flee. I sent up prayers for the former. I didn't think I could survive the latter.

I slowly shook my head, unable to look away. If I spoke, I'd break the spell, I was sure of it. And never in my life had I wanted something to happen so badly. Thumbs began to move again and I would have rejoiced, if I'd had any strength left in my body. Those shivers turned into full body jolts starting at my core and extending out to my extremities.

Somehow Kai was now towering over me, his hands still gripping my thighs, thumbs dancing up and down my slit, making me lose all thought of anything but the feel of his hands touching my most intimate spot.

I was left unsatisfied and turned on beyond belief as his hands left my thighs and reached up to peel my tank top off. My arms went willingly, but as soon as the cool air hit my skin, I crossed my arms over my body, feeling highly self-conscious. I needed it to be darker. Rolls and wobbly bits and stretch marks were typically overlooked in the darkness. Here was this hot life-guard, in fantastic physical shape, stroking my body and looking his fill.

Kai grabbed my wrists and brought his lips to mine. The kiss was sweet and innocent before he kicked it up a notch and invaded my mouth, tongues tangling. He was still attacking my mouth when he pulled my arms away from my body, his torso settling on top of me.

"Touch me, Ono," he whispered against my lips before diving in for more.

I didn't need to be told thrice to do something I'd dreamt of doing. I let my hands wander over his shirt, underneath to his warm skin, pushing his shirt up. He broke the kiss to whip the shirt off and throw it to the floor. Then he was back on top of me, kissing the side of my neck. I'd forgotten the luxurious feel of a man's hard body laying skin-to-skin on top of me. The friction of his hard chest against my tender breasts was enough to make me forget about covering myself.

His kisses traveled lower, and my hands couldn't reach his hard ass any longer. I was about to complain when his mouth closed over one nipple, killing any coherent words from tumbling from my lips. Fire shot from my breast to my core, making me gasp and press my hips up into his torso. I looked down and saw his dark hand full with my white breast, thumb back to sweeping across the tip, mimicking the flicking of his tongue on my other breast.

I gripped his head, my hands holding him to my breasts, wanting more friction. He complied, flicking faster, sucking harder. Teeth grazed, the pleasure-pain wrenching a moan out of me. Then he released my nipple from his mouth with a loud pop.

He was breathing hard, his chest heaving, rubbing along my breasts with each inhale. "So I ask again: do you trust me, Hessa?" His voice was nothing like I'd heard before from him; gravely and restrained, the musical quality nowhere to be found in his need.

"Yes. Yes, I trust you." I would say or do just about anything right now, which was also a new feeling for me. Sex was usually such a mechanical undertaking, a way to reach a physical release. We still had clothes on and already I felt more connected to Kai than I'd ever felt with past partners.

"Thank God," Kai breathed. Then he lifted off of me, reaching down to peel my shorts from my legs, baring me completely.

"Could-- Could we turn the lights off first?" I was back to feeling self-conscious in my body, knowing I was far from the bikini clad young things that I was sure threw themselves at him daily at his job. The Beach Squad was helping me accept my body more than before, but I'd need a lot of work before I pranced around naked any time soon.

Kai was sitting back on his heels, eyes roaming up and down my body. "Hell no, woman. I want to see every inch of you. Touch every inch. Kiss every inch. Memorize every inch. It's like your body was made for a man's pleasure. And since I'm the one you trust, I intend to take my pleasure. But I also believe in ladies first. You're going to want to see it all too, so the lights stay on."

I was gobsmacked. Kai wasn't a man to lie, no matter what, so if he said he loved my body, I had to believe he really did. Before I could analyze the situation further, he'd jumped up and started stripping off his shorts. Laces untied, velcro ripped open. Hands pushed down the shorts, dropping them to the floor.

And I thanked Thomas Edison with every cell in my body.

Hell yes, the lightbulbs were staying on. I couldn't take my eyes off the most beautiful erection I'd ever had the pleasure of seeing. It was standing tall, a slight curve leading to a head I was sure my mouth needed to feast on. It bobbed slightly as Kai walked his way over to me. I lifted off the armrest and reached out to grab hold.

Kai pulled back just out of my grasp. "What do you say, Ms. Woodland?"

Sure, I'd play his game. The reward was worth it. "Please?" I looked up at him, begging with my eyes.

He smirked. "It was the impeccable manners that got me. Just so you know."

It was infuriating having your own snark tossed in your face, but I had a gorgeous erection in my face too, so I was willing to overlook it. Kai moved back within reach, letting me finally get my hands on him. I stroked down his length, the baby soft skin a delicious juxtaposition with the hardness underneath.

My mouth opened, tongue snaking out to lick the tip. His taste filled my mouth, urging me to consume more. I held the base while I swirled my tongue over the head, thanking myself for indulging in every ice cream cone over the years. I'd indulged in plenty, as my hips would attest, and my mouth knew exactly what to do with the deliciousness offered up in the form of erection heaven. Kai moaned above me, letting me know he appreciated my ice cream cone skills as well.

I'd barely started when he pulled out of my mouth with a loud hiss. I pouted my lips, probably looking exactly like a kid who'd dropped their cone. One minute delight, the next devastation.

"Ladies first, remember?" Kai was breathing hard again, which made me feel slightly mollified. He reached down and pulled me up off the couch. "Jump up."

My eyes about bugged out of my head. "Pardon?"

"Jump up and put your legs around me. Let's take this into the bedroom where we have more room." He was pulling me into him, hands going under my arms in preparation for the jump that wasn't going to happen.

"Um, no thank you. Let's ambulate instead." There was no way in hell I was jumping on the poor guy. I wanted him fully functioning, not crumbling under the weight of my previous ice cream indulgences. Lights on plus picking me up? Was he trying to hit on all my insecurities in one go?

He tilted his head. "Seriously, Hessa? I carry fully grown men out of the ocean on a daily basis. You think I can't handle carrying you to your bedroom? You're like half my weight."

I scoffed. "Hardly! We probably weigh the same, but that's beside the point. Why not walk since we have perfectly functioning legs?"

"Are we seriously going to argue about this right now?" Kai pressed his body into mine, his erection reacquainting itself with my body. The reminder of that perfect appendage waiting to do wonderful things to me did make our argument seem a little silly.

I sighed. Nothing for it. It had to be done.

"Brace yourself."

Kai laughed but caught me easily when I jumped up and wrapped my legs around his waist. "See? I'll even reward you for trusting me again." His head bent and he sucked a nipple into his mouth, tongue driving me crazy. I couldn't help but grind up against his length, quickly finding the perfect spot for friction.

We were moving, our exact whereabouts beyond my comprehension, but when string lights lit up the dark, I realized we'd reached my bedroom. I'd foregone the typical ceiling fan light or bedside lamp options, instead wanting dim mood lighting.

Kai lifted his head away from my breast, taking in my room. "Nice lights."

"Thanks. Better for reading on my tablet in bed." Reading myself to sleep was how I operated, even as a young child. Reading was the most enthralling, yet relaxing thing I could do to unwind each night. Last thing I wanted was a spotlight in my eye.

"Sorry." Kai laid me back on the bed, following me down.

I wrinkled my nose. "For what?" He didn't look particularly sorry about anything.

"You won't be getting any reading done tonight."

Then his mouth went back to my breasts, a hand finding its way between my legs. What he didn't know was that I wouldn't need my book boyfriend tonight when I had the real thing bringing the words to life.

And that was the last coherent thought I had for awhile.

Kai spent copious amounts of time on my lips and my breasts, just teasing the part of me that wanted him the most. We eventually rolled over, landing me on top of him, in a position to lead this make-out session. But Kai had other ideas.

"Climb up here, legs on either side of my head, hands on the backboard," he barked.

The fog I'd been in made it hard to comprehend what he wanted. I started crawling up his body, not yet realizing what position his instructions would put me in. It was as I was placing each knee over his shoulders that I discovered what his intentions were.

A thrill ran through me even as I blushed fiery red.

"Kai..." I wasn't sure about this.

He looked up at me, burning me with his intensity. "Sit, woman." His hands grabbed my ass, pulling me down onto his face. My hands flew to the headboard to keep from falling over from the instant onslaught.

He fucked like he kissed. Lips and tongue attacking, flicking, nothing off-limits. I only worried for a moment I was going to smother him. Then I couldn't stop my hips from bucking on his face, wanting more, needing release. My body told my manners to go to hell and they fled like the scared little pansies they were. I'd apologize later if I restricted his air. This was fucking hot, demanding the entirety of my attention.

His tongue zeroed in on my clit, flicking relentlessly as he sucked it into his mouth. Then he rubbed his chin along my slit, his beard scruff scraping delightfully, before his soft tongue reappeared. My thighs shook, threatening to buckle when the orgasm hit. I gripped the headboard with all the strength I had, desperate to ride out the wave without actually smothering him with my entire body weight. Hard to do when you couldn't feel anything but white-hot pleasure between your legs.

His mouth continued its assault, slowing the pace enough to allow me to survive. When the last tremor left my body, Kai grabbed my torso and tilted me over to lay back next to him on the bed. I was boneless, allowing him to situate me however he wanted.

I used to play Raggedy Ann with my sister in the back of the car growing up. When my mom would turn, we'd flop to the side, crushing each other and invariably bursting into laughter at having no ability to hold ourselves upright.

This was a markedly better version of Raggedy Ann.

"What's so funny, gorgeous?" Kai was up on one elbow watching me giggle, which was cut off immediately at the sight of his wet chin.

I was still on his face. Oh, Lordy. Cue the full body blush.

"Do I even want to know what's going on in there?" Kai rapped his knuckles gently against the top of my head.

"Prolly not," I answered, unable to form a full sentence quite yet. I reached over and wiped his chin, unable to stand it any longer. He just grinned and rolled back on top of me.

This time when he kissed me, I tasted myself mixed with his own taste. It shouldn't have been a turn on, but it was, waking up parts of me that only moments ago thought they'd never recover. He took his time again, just playing and teasing. Not in any hurry to get to the main event, which left me happy but befuddled. Usually men were all about getting to the finish line as quickly as possible. What else was there?

I didn't have to wonder long as Kai began to rub his cock against me, teasing me with just a taste of the friction I needed. I bucked my hips seeking him out, hoping to prolong the sensations spiraling out to the rest of my body with each pass. My hands gripped his back, pulling him to me tightly. His chest rubbed along my breasts, adding to the thrill. I closed my eyes. I was so close.

Cold air hit me as Kai pushed away from me and climbed off the bed.

"W-where are you going?" He couldn't leave me like this. That would be cruel and unusual punishment. Yes, I'd already had one orgasm, but I was discovering I was a greedy bitch.

He reached down to the floor, giving me a view of the side of one sculpted glute muscle. I hadn't noticed how fine his backside was, so distracted was I by the impressive erection previously. As much as I wanted his body on top of me, pressing me into the bed, I also wanted to sit back and ogle him from afar. The boy was gorgeous. Long muscular legs, a tight ass, narrow hips, and wide shoulders. His skin was smooth and beautiful and the tan lines showed exactly where he wore his swim trunks at work.

"Want me to pose?" His voice pulled my eyes back up to his smirking face. Guess he caught me gawking.

"Yes, please." Why deny it?

He chuckled and came back over to the foot of the bed. Without speaking, he grabbed my ankles and pushed my legs apart in one forceful move, leaving me exposed to his gaze. His face hardened and as his eyes settled on my nether regions, I felt a trickle leak down, giving him even more to see. At that sight he didn't waste time crawling up the bed to settle between my legs.

I didn't think I'd ever been truly fucked before. Those interludes were too perfunctory and clinical to call fucking. I was guessing I'd finally be well and truly fucked before the night was over. My body clenched in anticipation, wanting it more than I ever thought I would.

Condom on, Kai lifted my knees up and out, holding me open for him. I didn't have time to be embarrassed as he plunged forward, filling me to the hilt. I gasped, loving the fullness, realizing for the first time that I'd been missing this exact feeling my whole life.

"Okay?" Kai was looking at me with concern.

"Oh, yes," I managed to whisper back. I was the okay-est I'd ever been.

The moment the words were out, he pulled back and thrust back in, setting a blistering pace. I reached behind me to the headboard and held on. This was nothing like I'd ever felt before. The sensations washing over my body were too strong, too forceful to be contained. My head thrashed back and forth on the pillow as I fought to control the impending explosion.

"Give it to me, Ono." Kai's voice was just a hoarse whisper now, his control almost as gone as mine. His hand left my knee and flicked clumsily across my clit, just enough pressure to set me off again.

I pressed my head back into the pillow and let the orgasm take me, not entirely sure I'd survive it. I was panting, eyes squeezed shut. Pops of color exploded across my eyelids and my nose went tingly.

Kai kept thrusting before suddenly stopping, dropping his head to my shoulder and gripping the pillow under my head. His harsh moan filled my ears, bringing a smug smile to my face.

He may have been the one thrusting, but I did that to him. I made him lose control. In my most vulnerable, naked state, I now felt the most powerful.

13

ai

I'm not sure what I expected from Hessa, but her ready ability to let go and give over to pleasure made me fall just a bit further into... Well, let's just say 'like' for the time being. I wasn't ready to analyze that thought any further before I had a chance to talk to her about us and where she wanted things to go. I was certain where I wanted things to go and the mind-blowing sex was a huge step forward to my ultimate goal.

When we woke up the next morning, she was pressed up against me, one leg sprawled across my hips, completely naked. All thoughts of sleep left as I took in her breasts, rising and falling gently as she slept peacefully. Her hand was dangerously close to touching my hard-on, which had experience a quick wake-up call.

Instead, I laid there and watched her as she slept. It seemed her mind was constantly going: thinking, analyzing, and searching for the perfect word or witty exchange. At least in sleep, she looked calm and relaxed, getting a chance to shut that brain down and recharge.

When she finally fluttered her eyes open, she looked confused at first, probably wondering who the warm body next to her belonged to.

"Oh, hi," she whispered. She gave me a sleepy grin, snuggling closer, which did in fact, put her hand on my hard-on. She gasped, realizing the situation.

"Good morning, beautiful. How'd you sleep?" My hand traveled down the length of her body, keeping her leg hooked over me, even as she tried to pull it back.

"Mmm...very good, thank you." She rubbed her eyes and then rolled out of my arms to stand up by the bed. She grabbed a shirt on the nightstand and put it on, covering her delicious curves, much to my disappointment.

"Where you going? Come back to bed." No school, no work. Why were we rushing to get out of bed?

"No, thank you. I have a bunch of work to do today. Thanks for last night though." She wasn't even looking at me, instead rushing about the room grabbing clothes. If this was a brush-off, which it sure as hell felt like, I was going to be pissed. Guess we'd have to have that serious talk sooner rather than later.

I also rolled out of bed and threw on my clothes, hurrying to catch up to her as she walked out of the bedroom. Anger and fear felt like a brick in my stomach as I followed her into the kitchen where she turned on the coffeepot. I'd finally found a woman I was interested in exploring a relationship with and she was giving me the brush-off. Was she not there last night? Did she not feel that instant connection from the very moment we laid eyes on each other?

I spun her around, backing her into the counter, purposefully invading her personal space. If she was going to send me on my way, she'd have to do it with her body pressed against mine and my eyes trained on hers to catch the lie. Her breath hitched at the contact, the first sign she was more affected by me than she was willing to admit.

"What gives, Hessa?"

Her face turned pink and her eyes tried to dart away from my stare. "Nothing gives. I just have things to do. Last night was fun, but I gotta get a move on."

"Fun? Last night was a lot of things, but even I could think of a lot more appropriate words before I landed on 'fun'. Last night was incredible, possibly life changing. So before you kick me out the door, we're going to talk about it. That okay by you?" I was trying hard to remember to breath in and out. Breathe in patience, breathe out anger.

Her eyes flew back to my face, and I could feel her spine straightening, leaving her rigid against me. "Listen Kai, I really like you, but let's be realistic. We just aren't compatible, so the sooner we acknowledge that, the better. We had some fun, but this isn't something long-term, so why are you mad?"

Well holy shit, she actually believed that bullshit. I closed my eyes and counted to ten. I knew anything said in anger wouldn't help the situation, but this woman was testing my calm nature. What I knew more than anything was that she was running scared. I'd seen a few of my friends go through it and laughed at their distress at the time. Now I was thankful for the insight.

When I had myself under control, I opened my eyes and cupped her face with my hands. Her eyes opened wide, unsure where I was going with this. I had her attention finally and I was going to make myself clear.

"What I know, Hessa, is that we're so compatible you're scared out of your mind. We both want something long-term and that want is so intense you think you have to shut me out now before you get hurt, because it couldn't possibly work out. Well, guess what, Ono? I'm not going anywhere. I'm going to prove to you exactly how good we are together, both now and forever. So run if you'd like, but I'll chase you down. Mark my word."

Then I kissed her quickly, released her, and went to grab my things. When I was on my way out the door, she still hadn't moved away from the counter, just staring out the kitchen window, deep in thought. I was hoping those thoughts would lead her to the same conclusion I had about our relationship, but if I knew Hessa, which I believed I did, it would take further convincing before she changed her stubborn mind.

Hessa

I went into school Monday morning, my stomach a mess of nerves about the day ahead of me and another feeling I couldn't put a name to. If I had to guess, it was a loathsome mix of sad, lonely, scared, and disappointed. I'd stayed busy all day Sunday in a vain attempt to keep my brain from analyzing where each of those emotions came from. I had a sneaking suspicion I was more than a little pissed off at myself, but chose to remain steadfast in my practicality and focus on my job instead.

I had just entered the main hallway of the high school when the admin office door opened and our school secretary called me over. Her face didn't hold its normal cheer. When her eyes wouldn't meet mine as I got closer, I acknowledged this wasn't a good sign. I followed her through the maze of small meeting rooms till we got to the Principal's door. She opened it and gestured for me to go in.

Mr. Brown was seated behind his desk, furiously pecking out an email. How a man could be the head of a school and still not know how to type properly was beyond me. He flung a hand out, which I guessed was an invitation to sit in one of the chairs in front of his desk. I had a seat, propped my bag exploding with the papers I'd graded over the weekend on the floor next to me and waited.

My mind wandered and I began to do what I did anytime I was overwhelmed: I wrote a song. Nerves don't make for good song lyrics though and I'd barely gotten past 'Mr. Brown and his frown, Hessa's going down' when the man himself spun in his chair and folded his hands on his desk.

I stifled the hysterical chuckle bubbling up in my throat and smoothed out my skirt with my sweaty palms.

"Ms. Woodland. Thank you for coming in before class. I've spoken with our district's lawyers over the weekend and they've assured me that the information from the police department is consistent with your claim of innocence."

He paused, giving me time to stab his beady, little eyes out with a sharp number two pencil, even if only in my imagination. My claim? Innocence? Was I on trial here and didn't know it? If the police had backed me up, it wasn't a 'claim' at all anymore, it was simply the truth.

He cleared his throat and continued, oblivious to my seething anger beneath the surface. "Be that as it may, we've decided to cancel the Care Dare program after this year. We'll have an assembly today right before lunch and announce the cancellation of the program, along with information regarding Gabe Martinez to calm any rumors. I'd like you to also warn the students not to get involved with online daring games. We'll be a united front and demonstrate we take this incident seriously." He spun back to his computer, dismissing me before I'd had a chance to process his deplorable demands.

I shook my head, wondering if he had any compassion at all. "What about Ms. Martinez? Gabe?"

He turned his head to look back at me, his annoyance at my questions clear on his face. "What about them?"

My jaw dropped. "Gabe is one of our students. We need to help him and his mother in their time of need!"

He flung his ridiculous hand again, clearly unperturbed by my outburst. "We're not responsible for what happened, Hessa."

I jumped up. "You're missing the point entirely! He needs help. Not being responsible does not absolve us from our obligation to provide assistance."

He smirked as he began pecking away at another blasted email. "You're welcome to help them if you feel so inclined."

I stared at his head, hoping my eyes would drill right into his skull and knock some sense into him. With no such luck, I grabbed my tote bag and huffed my way out of the room, not bothering to shut the door nicely. Mr. Brown's assistant startled at the slamming of the door and gaped at me, never having seen me in a tizzy before.

I used my meditation breaths to calm myself as I walked to my first class of the day. My mind tried to wander off to visions of Kai and his hard body above me, consuming me, but I willed the daydream away. I'd address that mess later. Right now, I had to come up with a plan to help my student.

Mr. Brown looked out at our student body, having given his announcement about 'the unfortunate incident relating to one of our beloved students'. He followed up that farce with the cancellation of the Care Dare program as of next school year. Whispers and shouts of disappointment echoed through the gymnasium as Mr. Brown tried to regain control.

"Now, now..." he said into the microphone, his voice gaining volume as he continued. "We have one more announcement for you and you'll want to hear this one, so settle down. Ms. Woodland?" He turned to me, stepping back from the podium.

I walked from my chair to the microphone, ignoring the pretense of a friendly smile from Mr. Brown as he took his seat behind me.

I looked out over the faces of my students, seeing the gamut of emotions: boredom, concern, anger, and confusion. As I was about to start my hastily prepared speech, the side doors opened and a tall, gorgeous woman walked in, followed by Kai. My heart jumped and quickly plummeted, seeing how quickly he'd moved on. Then my own confusion set in as I wondered what he was doing here. Mr. Brown cleared his throat and I rushed to begin, tracking the pair as they sat in the front row of the bleachers off to the side.

"Students. I'm as sad as you are to cancel our Care Dare tradition. I'm sorry this is the last senior class that gets to hone their interviewing skills. Or dig deep to find the bravery to try something new. Or learn the exultant feeling of accomplishing something you thought was beyond your capabilities. I will be working tirelessly to create a new program our seniors can look forward to each year. In the meantime, I ask that you be vigilant. Guard your social media and remember that no legit dares will be given publicly. If you find yourself dared to do something dangerous online, do the right thing. Tell your parents, tell a teacher. Whatever you do, do not put yourself in danger by accepting an online dare."

I paused to collect my thoughts. This next bit might endanger my job and make me a fool publicly, but it was the right thing to do. I asked my seniors to push beyond their limits. Time I did too.

"Lastly, I'd like to invite you to a night of singing under the stars at an establishment yet to be determined in HB. Your favorite English teacher will be singing to all who gather sometime next month. I'll be releasing the details shortly. I will be collecting a $10 cover charge, 100% of which will go to the medical bills of our student in the hospital. I encourage you all to come watch me make a fool of myself and enjoy a fall night together."

The murmuring started up again with quite a few students shouting their encouragement to me. I smiled but it felt wooden, stiff with fear. My legs were shaking as I made my way back to collapse in my chair.

There. I'd said it. No going back now.

I glanced up and caught Kai's eye. He was staring at me intently. He nodded slowly, recognizing what my announcement meant to me. He of all people knew how terrified I was to sing in public. That simple nod made the disappointed feeling come to the forefront yet again. I rubbed my chest, hoping to sooth the ache that had started up there. I'd had my chance with this wonderful man and I'd pushed him away. Based on the woman next to him, my window of opportunity was closed. So why was he here? Other than to rub my face in how quickly he'd replaced me.

While Mr. Brown dismissed the students, I saw Kai and the woman jump up and make their way through the crowd. Before I could run from the gym, they intercepted me.

"Hessa!" Kai caught my arm, bringing me to a halt, forcing me to acknowledge the woman I hated on sight. She was tall with curly brown hair, artfully tossed up in an up-do, leaving her classically beautiful face on display for all to admire. For cripes sake, she looked like Wonder Woman in a pantsuit, basically, the opposite of everything I was. I felt fatter and frumpier by the second next to this elegant, stunning woman. It didn't help that Kai seemed to know her well, based on his hand on her back as they stood together. As if this day couldn't get any shittier.

I pasted a wide smile on my face, determined not to let my true feelings bleed through and embarrass me entirely. No reason to look like a sad sap. I stuck my hand out, ready to get this introduction out of the way. "Hi, I'm Hessa Woodland."

She grabbed my hand in a firm shake. "Lovely to meet you. I'm Fiona, a reporter for the HB Republic. Mind if we find a more private spot to chat?"

Oh sure, just what I wanted. To hang with her and Kai in a private spot, just the three of us. Like a third wheel. Like an awkward three-legged stool. I could see which one of us was losing in this love triangle.

Instead of turning tail and running away like every fiber of my being wanted to do, I kept that smile going, promising my cheeks some extra ice cream tonight if they just held it together a bit longer. I led us over to the corner of the gym where we wouldn't be interrupted.

I nearly jumped out of my heels when I felt Kai's hand come to rest on my back, just grazing my booty with each step I took. I shot him a look, but he wasn't looking at me, oblivious to my distress.

What was his game? Come with one woman, leave with another? For all I knew, maybe I was the interloper. He may have already been dating Fiona and just kept me a secret this weekend. But before I could come up with any other scenarios to explain his behavior, we'd reached the corner and Fiona pulled a notebook out of her bag.

"I hope you don't mind. Kai called me up and said there was a story here that needed to be covered and I have to agree. Can you first tell me about the Care Dare program?" Fiona didn't waste any time getting down to business, which I appreciated. The sooner I could leave and organize my thoughts in private, the better for all parties present.

I ignored Kai and told her all about the program. Then I told her about the online dares that had been happening, ending with Gabe's accident and the Principal's decision to shut down the program.

"Kai also told me that you were personally dared. Is that right?" Fiona was furiously scribbling on her notepad. I glanced over to Kai, who stood there looking at me with a tender smile, like things weren't awkward between us at all.

Then he quirked an eyebrow and his eyes heated. The exact expression I'd seen right before he climbed between my legs Saturday night took over his face, completely derailing my train of thought. My face began to blush, remembering all that had happened that night.

"Hessa?" Fiona was looking at me like I'd lost the plot. Her pen was hovering over her notebook, waiting for me to answer her questions.

"Pardon?" My voice came out breathless. Damn Kai and his sex looks.

Fiona asked again patiently. "Tell me about your own dare."

I focused on her entirely, pretending Kai wasn't there, and told her the whole story.

"Kai also gave me a quote about the happenings at the beach. Do you mind if I include in my article an invitation to your fundraiser next month?" Fiona asked innocently.

That sounded like my worst nightmare. More people to watch me humiliate myself? Sure, why not? Let's bus 'em in from surrounding cities while we were at it.

Kai finally spoke up. "Hessa, Fiona thinks this article, along with your fundraiser, will draw a lot of attention to the good things you're doing here with the Care Dare program. I think we may even be able to get it reinstated next year once the public sees it has nothing to do with the online dares." Then he reached out and held my hand, dropping his voice. "I know you're scared to do it, but this could be a really good thing for your program. And think of all the money raised for Gabe."

I sighed. Dammit, he knew how to get me to agree. "Fine. It can go in the paper, but if I have to move cities to escape the humiliation, you're helping me pack up all my things."

Kai chuckled before pulling me in and kissing my forehead. "For you? Anything," he whispered.

Fiona chucked her notebook back in her bag and shook my hand again. "You've got a good one here. His idea to get this in the paper was brilliant. Plus, I get a feel good story. Win-win. See ya' around, Hessa."

I watched her walk off, mouth agape. I spun back to Kai.

"I'm confused. What just happened?"

Kai still had my hand hostage, so he pulled me close and kissed me quickly. "I'm supporting you. Jack called me last night after he talked to your Principal about today's assembly and cancelling the program. I know your students are a priority for you, so I thought publicly highlighting what you're doing here would not only raise more money for Gabe's recovery, but also give you a chance at saving your Care Dare program. If enough people get behind it, they'll complain that it's being cancelled. Your Principal will be forced to bring it back. Fiona wrote an article awhile back about Esa's shop and her stalker. I figured she'd like your story too."

That was brilliant, just like Fiona said. And really damn sweet. It actually seemed exactly like something Kai would do, so I'm not sure why I was surprised. Or why I was pushing him away.

"I gotta get back to work, so I'll call you tonight." Kai kissed me again and walked off, leaving me alone with my scattered thoughts.

14

essa

All week, Kai called and texted me, acting like we were together. A couple.

And it was nice.

We talked about everything and nothing, no topic too silly to discuss. I shared a bit about my mom, my sister, and the genre of books I read at night when all my papers were graded. I learned more about his family, the way he grew up, what he did in his spare time. We bonded over the fact that we'd had divorced parents. He hated being separated from his dad for such long periods of time. I believed him when he said he wanted to be around every single day for his kids, when that time came.

We never discussed our relationship or where we stood. It was all about getting to know each other and developing a deeper level of comfort with each other. We'd already been intimate, but I felt closer to him now, knowing who he was underneath all the tan and muscles and gorgeousness.

Friday night came quickly without any further run-ins with my Principal, and I was looking forward to a night of pajamas the moment I walked through my door. In my estimation, a frozen burrito, some light music, and a good book were the ingredients for a perfect night.

I was jammed up, as Esa would say, when my doorbell rang. I groaned, the first bite of burrito taunting me from my untouched plate, fresh out of the microwave. A quick look in the peephole showed my sister standing on my doorstep holding a plant.

I swung open the door and let her in, apologizing for my state of undress. She laughed me off and shoved the pot in my hands.

"Here. A housewarming gift." She breezed into my living room, leaving me to find a spot for my newly acquired plant.

When I made it to the living room, sans plant, I found her wolfing down my burrito.

"Oopth. Thorry, wa da for ou?" she mumbled with her mouth full of bean burrito deliciousness.

"I live alone, Rainna. Who else would it be for?" I crossed my arms, leaning against the doorway. "To what do I owe the pleasure of your company this fine evening?" A sickly sweet smile split my face as I unleashed my irritation in the form of sarcasm.

She wiped her mouth with the 'Books Are Life' napkin I'd meticulously placed under my plate earlier. "Well, I missed your actual housewarming a few years back, so I thought I'd remedy that now. Hence, the plant."

Okay, that was kind of nice. A lot nice. I dropped the false smile and flopped down on the couch next to her.

"Thank you. That's really thoughtful. I'll probably kill it with my black thumb in a matter of days, but the thought is very nice." I gave her a quick hug. "So what's new with you, sister dearest?" I hopped off the couch and waved at her to follow me into the kitchen. My stomach growled right on cue.

"I don't have a client till ten p.m. so I thought we could just hang out for a bit." She sat on a bar stool and watched me heat another burrito.

"Sounds good to me. I didn't have anything planned except relaxing." My phone buzzed with a new text on the counter. I leaned over and saw it was from Kai. I swiped it open and read it, quickly typing a reply and sending.

Rainna whistled. "Who's got you blushing and smiling like that, huh?" Then she began to sing-song like only an annoying sister could. "Hessa's got a new boyfriend...Hessa's got a new boyfriend."

"Shut it, woman!" I was embarrassed to be caught in the act, like a naughty teenager, but I really wanted to share my excitement with my sister. The microwave dinged, so I took the burrito and went back into the living room, Rainna trailing me.

"Details, give me details."

"Let me eat first and then I'll tell you everything you want to know. Wait. Almost everything."

"Ooooh! Those kind of details, huh? I can't wait." Rainna sat on the floor across from the coffee table and waited not-so-patiently for me to inhale my burrito. Her eyes sparkled and her skin glowed. She looked good, which was nice to finally see.

I took my time with the last bite, making sure to chew it at least one hundred times before swallowing, and then wiping my mouth thoroughly. Rainna glared at me, knowing I was doing it just to annoy her. Then the doorbell rang again and I laughed out loud at her expression.

"Nooooo!" she whined. I hopped up and looked through the peephole again, seeing a crowd on my doorstep.

"Prepare thyself!" I yelled back to Rainna. I swung the door open a second time that night and let in the circus. Also known as the Beach Squad.

After all the introductions were done, I opened the bottles of wine the girls brought and handed out wineglasses. Rainna declined, opting for water instead, which impressed me. I didn't have enough furniture for everyone, so half of us settled on the floor with minimal squabbling.

Bailey leaned over to me while the girls were still shouting over each other about the nuances of white versus red wine and passed me an envelope. "I looked into that thing we talked about. Found some interesting things. But remember, I had nothing to do with the information you have there. Got it?"

I took the envelope, winked my acceptance, and put the envelope on my counter to be opened later when I was alone. I was curious to see what she'd found, but knew there was nothing I could do about it right this minute, anyway. I'd look at it tonight, sleep on it, and then approach Jack with the information if I felt it would help the investigation.

As soon as I sat back down, Esa shushed everyone and all eyes landed on me.

"What?" I asked, bewildered.

"You've got some 'splaining to do, Lucy!" Shasta said with a ridiculous Ricky Ricardo accent.

"That was bad, real bad," Bailey muttered into her wineglass.

"Let me give you some background here. We were all at Chocolate Dreams on Wednesday. So were our favorite lifeguards. Two things stood out for us. One, you announced to the whole world you'd sing in public and didn't tell us...and this was after saying you'd never do it. Two, Kai seems pretty hung up on you and you haven't given us the goods." Brinley brought me up to speed on why they were looking at me expectantly.

"I always thought Kai was pretty damn hot, but it was clear from the way he was talking about you, he's already taken," Autumn admitted shyly. She smiled at me so I knew she didn't hold any grudges. Her words made my tummy flip-flop with excitement. I didn't know for sure if Kai was actually mine, but the idea was starting to appeal to me more than scare me.

Shasta broke it down for me. "Maybe we weren't clear enough, but here in the Squad, we tell each other everything. We lean on each other. If you can't lean on us, then we feel slighted, plain and simple. You haven't taken that opportunity yet, so we've come to you."

My good mood plummeted. I never meant to hurt their feelings. I guess things just happened quickly the last week or so and I didn't think to update them. "I'm so sorry, you guys." That's all I got out before my eyes filled with tears and I jammed my lips together to keep my emotions in check.

Rainna rubbed her hand on my back and spoke for me. "Hessa here has always been the responsible one. She doesn't lean on other people because she's always the one who has to pick up the pieces for everyone else. Maybe you could give her an out, just this once, while she learns how to rely on good friends?"

"Of course we can!" Esa was quick to say. "Listen, we've all gone through rough patches or issues with men, and we've got to be able to rely on each other during those times to stay sane. If you shut us out, we don't know how to help you. And I guarantee you that every woman needs a group of women to back her up in life. We want to be your back up. So spill, woman."

I swallowed through a thick throat and did just that, telling them everything that had happened with my student, the Principal, the reporter, and finally, Kai. I skipped the sexy-time details, feeling like some things were too sacred to go blabbing about, even with the best of friends. When I'd finished unloading, we'd finished two bottles of wine and Bailey was reaching for another.

"Okay, first, let's get the boring stuff out of the way, then we'll get to the juicy details. I can help you with your fundraiser. Do it at Pacific City, in the downstairs courtyard. They have singers out there all the time. I'll set up a hot chocolate station and we'll donate the profits to your student. I can even talk to some other vendors there and see if they'll donate a portion of the night's proceeds to your cause." Esa grabbed a napkin and a pen from her bag and began to write down notes.

I felt a strange but welcome warmth bubbling up my body, making my heart race and my tear ducts flood. I couldn't believe I didn't even have to ask. Esa was just willing to pitch in and help. "I-I'd love that. Thank you so much!"

"If you make up some flyers, I can have them at the register at work," Bailey suggested.

"Oh! Us too. We can hand them out to our classes at Strike Ready," Brinley added.

I nodded my head, mind spinning with all we could do to pimp out the event to make the most money possible. If I focused on that, I wouldn't have to focus on the actual singing that I'd have to do the night of the event.

My head was ping-ponging back and forth between Esa and Bailey while they argued about what we should name the event. I had a smile on my face I couldn't seem to get rid of.

Shasta waved to get my attention. "See why you need to lean on friends? It's that feeling you got right there. The one that makes you feel like you're floating on air and can accomplish anything." She was grinning at me in a very motherly way. She was rough around the edges, but it was clear she really did want the best for all us girls. I nodded back, understanding exactly what she meant.

Rainna leaned over and wrapped an arm around me. "I'm so happy for you, Hessy. These friends of yours are the bomb," she whispered.

"They really are," I whispered back.

"Hey! Enough arguing already. Some of us are single here and we'd like to get to the sex stuff so we can live vicariously through you sluts, okay?" Autumn interrupted, getting a fist pump from Bailey.

Esa threw a napkin at Autumn, who threw it right back.

"You're just jealous," Brinley said smugly.

"Damn right we are!" Bailey shouted back, making us all laugh.

"I don't know why you're whining. I'm single, but I get plenty of sex. You're just doing single all wrong." Shasta swirled her wine, looking very much the sexy siren even though she was by far the oldest woman in the room. She was the perfect cougar.

Rainna whistled while the rest of us groaned. We didn't want to hear about Shasta's friends-with-benefits arrangements. We'd heard enough already since she was constantly chattering on about who her 'special friends' were. If I was on the one end of the spectrum with under-sharing, Shasta was on the far other end, that's for sure.

When everyone had settled down, I explained my reluctance to get involved any further with Kai. "I like the guy, but let's be real. He's a total hippie. He walks around barefoot most of the time, for cripes sake. Rainna can attest: we had a hippie for a father and I want nothing to do with that." Rainna nodded in agreement. "I really like Kai. I do. But long-term? I just don't see it working out."

"Hmm. Maybe I should take this one, guys," Brinley spoke up, eyebrows knitted. "Listen, Hessa. I had the world's worst father. Emotional and physical abuse the whole time growing up. Found out not long ago that he'd actually kidnapped me from my mother when I was an infant. Told me my whole life that my mom had passed away when I was a baby. I would never compare shitty parents, but I think I know where you're coming from with wanting to avoid getting involved with someone just like your father."

Wow. I'd had no idea she'd gone through all that. My father was just absent from my life. Her's sounded far worse. Plus, I'd always had my mom. She hadn't.

"So what advice do you have for me?" I hoped she'd keep sharing.

"When Dean barreled his way into my life, I was very resistant. In fact, I was downright rude to him. I had a huge wall built and thankfully, he stuck around and helped me pull that wall down, brick by brick. Let your past help you make smart decisions, but don't let it hold you back from the best thing that could happen to you simply because you're scared. Share your concerns with Kai and see what he says. I bet you'll be surprised with what he says. He's a good guy, Hessa. One of the best."

I spoke slowly, thinking about what she'd said. "Truth be told, Kai's never done or said anything to make me feel that he'd be just like my father. I've just made assumptions that he would. Maybe I should give him a chance."

Brinley smiled and nodded. I still couldn't get over what she'd gone through, and I fully appreciated her sharing that with me tonight. I leaned across the carpet to give her a hug.

Everyone seemed happy with my decision. We all raised our wineglasses for a toast in friendship and then spent another hour just drinking, talking about clothes, men, and if we all wanted to try surfing together one day. Rainna and Brinley, the only two sober among us, decided we were hammered if we were making plans to surf. Everyone disbanded, placing wineglasses in the kitchen and grabbing purses, before making their way to my front door.

"For future reference, do you ya'll have like a phone tree or something?" I asked.

"A what?" Bailey asked, scrunching up her face.

"You know, like a diagram outlining who to call in case of an emergency and then it tells you who that person should call."

They all busted up laughing. "No, but that's a damn good idea. This group is getting unwieldy. That'll be your assignment, Hessa. Make us a phone tree, wouldya?" Shasta ordered.

After hugs all around, they left, leaving my apartment eerily quiet.

I left the glasses in the sink, promising myself to clean them first thing in the morning. I walked to my bedroom, memories of the night with Kai running through my brain. I looked at my bedframe where he'd told me to put my hands while he pleasured me from below.

Suddenly, I couldn't stand to go to bed all alone. I needed to talk to Kai and let him know I was all in. I wanted to give us another chance. Hell, I wanted another night together.

I figured I had just enough wine on board to do something stupid, so before I could back out, I put my plan in action. I texted him, asking for his house address, saying I had something to drop off to him. Then I whipped off my pajamas, spritzed myself with perfume, dabbed some smokey shadow on my eyelids, brushed out my hair, and added bright red lipstick. I slipped on a winter coat over my naked body and topped off the look with my black heels that Kai said he loved so much.

Time for Operation Get My Man Back.

15

essa

I knew I should have thought this thing through better. The coat I'd chosen looked sexy as hell, but it was a wool blend, scratchy enough in all the wrong places to leave me no option but to scratch myself like a major league baseball player. With my luck, by the time Kai got this thing off I'd have hives and attractive red splotches all over me. Plus it was chafing my nipples so badly I'd need a balm of some sort. Not that I'd ever seen a nipple balm in the Walgreens aisle. Maybe a thick lotion. No alcohol in it though. Damn, just the idea of burning nipples made me shiver.

I finally swung into a parking space just around the corner from his apartment. I was thankful for the darkness this late at night when I flashed all of Huntington Beach getting out of my low car. The cool air that flew up my coat felt good though on my itchy skin. I was overheating, thinking about what I was doing.

The alcohol was starting to wear off a bit, making me question my sanity with this ridiculous plan. It was too late to go back, so I grabbed my purse and locked the car. It shouldn't have taken me longer than a minute to walk to his door, but damn, all the doors looked the same in the dark. I ended up circling two of the apartment buildings twice, sinking one of my heels into the lawn on the latest unfortunate lap. It was as I was wrenching my heel out of the grass that I got spun around and saw the correct building. Heel recovered, lady bits covered, and destination in sight, I felt emboldened, ready to execute on the fun part of my plan.

Seduction, baby.

Standing in front of his door, I tried out a few poses before knocking, trying to find the right one that screamed 'take me to bed' without looking like I was trying too hard. Hand on hip? No. Feet together or wide apart? Wide felt weird, but again, the draft felt glorious on my feverish skin. Definitely wide. Facing forward or sticking my booty out and looking over my shoulder at him? Probably facing forward, giving him a view of the girls. Purse on shoulder or held in my hand? No, better for it to be down on the floor by my feet so it wouldn't get in the way of my pose.

A lightbulb moment had me leaning against the doorframe, other hand up in my hair. Totally carefree, right? I knocked, then quickly put my hand back up in my hair like he'd just caught me casually running my hands through my luscious locks.

The door flew open right as I arranged my face in the duck lips all the kids were doing these days.

"Hessa?" Kai was looking at me like he'd never seen me before.

I leaned forward to kiss him, but my shoulder slipped off the doorframe. My other hand was useless to aid in my recovery, seeing as how it was still locked in my hair, frozen in mid-pose. Likewise, my feet were useless as they were nice and wide, perfectly stable in case of a lateral push, but ineffective in a forward fall. I was falling, watching Kai's face transform in slow motion from confused and amused to horrified.

You know those moments that slow down and you know exactly the horrible thing that's about to happen, yet can do nothing to stop it? Yeah, that was me. Free falling to the floor, my seductive pose frozen in place, even as the ship went down.

Moments before I face-planted at Kai's feet, strong hands grabbed my body and instead of a wood floor, I felt hard muscle cushion my fall. I squeaked on impact, not sure whether to rejoice at the averted disaster or apologize for my embarrassing entrance.

Kai pulled me back to standing, which was no easy task, since I had very little mind-muscle connection going on and since my hand bag was now tangled up in my feet. Once I kicked off the bag like an offending piece of seaweed, sending it shooting across his hallway floor, I decided to go back to the original plan.

I assumed the position: feet planted wide apart, hand on hip and the other in my hair. Come to think of it, I was going to make this my new power pose. Start every class like this. Definitely start my public concert in this pose. I felt like I could take on the world as long as I hit this first.

"Hessa. What are you doing?" Kai had his hands on his hips too.

Looked like he had his own power pose going on. Mine was considerably more friendly though, if I did say so myself. His pose included a scrunched up face and an air of irritation. Well, now we just had a power pose stand-off going on. What was I supposed to do next? I'd only planned to show up and figured he'd have his way with me as soon as I walked in the door.

The first trickle of doubt creeped in. Perhaps a bit belated, and certainly surprising as most sane people would have started doubting the plan the minute they'd fallen through the doorway, but I was always optimistic. I'd been so confident that Kai would want me, ridiculous plan and all.

I flung my hands down to my sides, power pose forgotten in my distress. I turned to have a seat on his couch and explain myself. My ankle wasn't in on the plan though, rolling in my sky high shoes and nearly sending me back to the floor as my heel slid sideways on the slick wood floor.

"Jumpin' Jehoshaphat! Why is it so hard to stand up?" I'd caught myself, hanging onto the side table lining his hallway for dear life.

I heard a snicker from behind me and dared a slow pivot to see Kai's arms crossed over his chest, one hand pressed to his mouth suppressing his mirth.

I felt like the flames of Hades were licking up my legs, lighting my whole body on fire from the inside out. I was embarrassed and worn out from all the walking around outside and the near mishaps once inside. And the damn coat was feeling like a Brillo pad on every square inch of skin. To top it off, not only was Kai not attacking me like I'd planned, but he was now laughing. *At* me. Definitely not *with* me.

I dared the devil by taking one hand off the table and opening the collar of my coat to get some fresh air before I burst into flames. "It's hotter than a half-fucked fox in a forest fire around here," I mumbled to myself, desperately trying to come up with my next move.

My eyes shot up as Kai burst into laughter, doubling over, hand on his knee to hold himself upright.

If looks could kill, he would have re-thought his fit of laughter. I waited him out, figuring he wouldn't hear me over his howls of laughter. The fucker was hot even as he pissed me off. Against my will, my lips turned up at the sound of his laugh, finding it contagious. He finally straightened up, wiping his eyes before looking at me again.

"How much have you had to drink, Ono?" His voice was higher pitched than normal, as he tried to reign it in. I wanted to wipe that smirky little smile right off his face.

"Not much. Why?" My free hand went back on my hip, ready to defend my sobriety.

Kai came right up to me and lifted my chin, gazing into my

eyes. "Uh huh. Sure. How about we go sit down and I get you some water?"

Before I could respond, he bent down and lifted me up in a princess carry. I squeaked again, wondering how much he weight lifted in order to keep carrying me around like this. I ran a hand down his bicep involved in holding my legs, enjoying the firm, bubble of muscle I felt there. Before I could get too handsy, he placed me down on the sofa and removed my heels. Then he was walking away to get me water.

I gulped down the bottle he brought back, enjoying the slide of ice cold water down my heated throat.

"So let's start over. What are you doing here, Hessa?" Kai was sitting on the coffee table facing me, crowding my legs. His hands were on my knees. I was hoping we'd get back to the plan and he'd push my knees apart and find out what was, or wasn't, underneath my coat. Speaking of coat, I needed to get out of that thing ASAP.

Kai

I finally had her seated, my hands holding her in place. I was afraid she'd slide right off the sofa if I didn't take extra precautions. She'd flashed me when she'd almost fallen the second time, so I knew she was naked under that coat. I could piece together why she'd come over, but I needed to hear her say it. Needed to know if she was all in on this relationship. No more hot and cold.

She threw her empty water bottle behind the sofa with a careless toss. Guess she was done. I fought a smile, knowing laughing again would really piss her off. But damn. Drunk Hessa was a side I never thought I'd see, but so glad I did. She was funny as hell.

My smile vanished quickly when I saw her untie her coat belt, pushing the collar off her shoulders.

"Wait--" I was going to stop her, knowing she was in no condition for what she was determined to come here and do. But the bright red of her skin had me pausing.

I leaned forward getting right up next to her neck and collarbone. Her skin was a red, mottled mess. "What the hell happened, Hessa?"

"Huh?" She opened her eyes, looked down where I was looking and saw her skin. "Oh, it was just rubbing and it's so hot..."

"Yeah I know, hotter than a half-fucked fox in a forest fire?"

She gasped, jaw dropping comically. "Yes! How'd you know?"

I shook my head, focusing on sliding the coat off her body, seeing that the rash was all over. "Babe, we gotta get this coat off you."

"I like the way you think, hot stuff," she said in a slurred, sexy purr. Her eyes were almost completely closed, a smile on her face.

"No, Hessa. I think you have a rash from your coat. We gotta get this off you right now." I managed to get her arms out and then I lifted her up, whipping the coat out from underneath her and throwing it on the floor, to the side of the sofa.

"Jesus, Ono," I whispered. Her whole body was covered in an angry red rash. My first aid training kicked in and I knew I needed to get some Benadryl in her system stat. "Stay right there, okay?"

She clucked, using one hand to give me an enthusiastic thumbs-up, one eye winking, then the other. She was a mess. An adorable mess.

I rushed to my bathroom and grabbed the Benadryl, measuring out a dose and racing back, hoping she hadn't slumped to the floor. I tilted her head back and got her to drink the medicine. I followed that up with the water left in my water bottle.

Then I scooped her up in my arms again. "Off to bed."

She wrapped her arms around me, eyes completely closed. I felt her lips pressed against my neck. Then her tongue darted out, licking me before she kissed me again. I couldn't help my body's response. The woman was a tease. I knew it couldn't go further as she'd be passed out asleep the moment I laid her down, but I was only human. She was naked in my house, licking my neck. Talk about temptation.

As predicted, by the time I laid her out in my bed and pulled the covers up, she was asleep, oblivious to my straining shorts. I kissed her forehead before turning to my bathroom. Time for a cold shower.

Hessa

I woke to someone pounding on my head. I tried to kick the covers off but they just tightened around me, pulling me back. I opened my eyes, blinking repeatedly trying to piece together where I was. Then I felt a hand travel up my stomach to grab hold of my naked breast and a steel rod pressed into my backside.

Like flashes of a movie reel, I saw glimpses of what happened last night run through my mind. Staring at the wall, I was both confused, horrified, and embarrassed. I gasped as that same hand traveled south, distracting me from my trip down memory lane. It stroked over my stomach, skated around Mt. Pleasant, and traced down my thigh.

"Kai!" Oh God, I'd have to apologize to him as soon as possible. I couldn't believe he saw me like that. I had no recollection of what happened after I almost fell a second time. A second time! Dear God, who the hell was that last night?

"Mmhmm," Kai groaned into my ear from behind me, his voice gravelly with sleep.

I ignored my throbbing head and turned in his arms. I needed to get this out before he kept feeling me up. "Kai?"

His eyes opened, showing me bright green irises. I brought my hand up to his face, finding his beard scruffy in the best way. The kind of scratchy that has a girl thinking of other places she wanted that beard. "Good morning," he whispered.

"Hi!" I cleared my throat, searching for better words. I wanted to leave inarticulate, drunk Hessa a distant memory. "I-I know I was a total mess last night and I'm so sorry. I'm not sure what all happened but it was inexcusable. Thank you for taking care of me."

He smiled, rubbing his hand along my arm, tracing his finger over my collarbone. "You were actually hilarious, but I am concerned still about your rash. Looks like the Benadryl knocked it out."

I looked down at my chest, confused. "Rash?"

"When I got your coat off, you were covered in a nasty rash. Have you worn that coat before?"

"I wore it once last winter, but with clothes on underneath." I blushed, remembering how I'd been naked the whole time.

Kai's smile got bigger. "Yeah, I really liked that. Maybe next time, don't use a wool coat.""

I huffed out a laugh. "There won't be a next time! I think I embarrassed myself enough."

His smile turned into a pout. "Will you at least wear the heels again? I really like the idea of you in the heels. And nothing else." He thrust his hips into mine, reminding me of our naked states.

"Does this mean you forgive me and we're good?"

"Depends. Does this mean you want a relationship with me? You agree that we'd be good together?" He wasn't going to let me off the hook easily, which I understood. I did brush him off pretty hardcore last time.

I wanted to be as honest with him as I could. "Absolutely. I'm still scared, but I'm willing to give you my best try."

The words had barely left my lips before he rolled on top of me, lips pressed to mine, sealing the deal. Then he pulled back, trapping my hands above my head, pressing my wrists into the soft mattress.

"Just so we're clear, nothing happened last night. I gave you Benadryl and put you to bed. I know you've been hesitant to take this further, but I've been clear from the beginning. You mean everything to me, Ono. I respect you and value you. I'll never take your trust in me for granted. And I'll never just walk away from you."

Having no words to respond, I lifted my head and kissed him instead, hoping it conveyed all I felt for this man.

He broke the kiss again, not yet done though he was breathing heavy. "There's a word in my culture called Ku'uipo. It means sweetheart. But it's stronger than the English equivalent of girlfriend. It means lover, best friend, the one you want by your side for a lifetime." He paused to search my eyes. "You're my Ku'uipo, Hessa."

There wasn't much more my wine marinated brain could handle. I had no witty reply, just tears as I realized how lucky I was to be in this man's life. He even kissed those away before moving down my body, waking up every part of me with lips, tongue, and teeth.

And when he filled me, bringing me over the edge, it wasn't his name I cried out. It was Ku'uipo.

16

essa

I discovered morning sex was the best cure for a hangover. It was sweet. It was slow. And it blasted through the remaining fuzz in my head. As we lay wrapped around each other in post-coital bliss, I listed out all the ways to say how I felt about him. Together, we came up with quite a few.

I was head over heels for Kai. Enamored. Boy crazy. Crushin' on him. Lovesick. Infatuated. Sweet on him. Basically, all the words and phrases that circled around what I was actually feeling for him: in love. I wasn't ready to say it yet. I wanted more time to just be together. The words would come later when I was absolutely certain. When I said it to him, I would mean it to the depths of my soul. I didn't take those three little words lightly. When I said it, it would be forever.

Saturday melted into Sunday. We drove to my house to pick up papers I needed to grade, along with some actual clothes. I couldn't keep wearing one of Kai's t-shirts with no undies. He said it was too distracting, but secretly, I think he loved the easy access. I struck a compromise by putting on a matching bra and lacy thong set Bailey had picked out for me at Nordstrom. If I couldn't be naked, I'd at least be in something better than worn out granny panties.

Kai had to run down to the garage to pick up his VW van. He'd had some repairs done to it and from the way he went on about it, I was excited to see it. He was my beach hippie, through and through. I was learning to love that about him, rather than equate it with something negative.

While he went to the garage, I sent a group text to the Beach Squad letting them know where I stood with Kai. I heard back instantaneous congratulations, along with several pleas for details on the sex. Those girls made me laugh.

I even updated my Instabook profile to 'In a Relationship'. Then I grabbed my laptop and formatted some fliers advertising my upcoming fundraiser concert. Esa got back to me saying she'd talked to the powers-that-be at Pacific City and she had the court-yard booked next month and several stores had already promised to pitch in.

Kai was grinning ear to ear when he came home, his VW keys swinging around his finger. In his other hand, he had a bag with Chinese take-out. We ate and talked all about his van. It was a vintage VW that hadn't had any work done on it for many decades. Kai was adamant about fixing it up to its former glory and taking us for drives up the coast of California. He said origi-nally he didn't care about fixing it up, but said he realized he needed a spruced up carriage for his princess. I eye-rolled hard at that line, but I did appreciate the fact that he was fixing it up. I didn't want to take drives with the engine breaking down and the springs in the seat poking me in the ass.

After we finished eating, Kai grabbed the keys again and pulled me out the door. We were going to do our meditation down at the beach, a habit I wanted to pick up from now on too.

We pulled up into a parking lot far south of the pier on the Huntington Beach State beach, parking the van so it faced the ocean with the side door open. I was impressed with the work that Kai had done on the vehicle so far. It looked clean and safe, so that was a relief. I'm sure all the decorative touches would come later. We sat down in the van, our legs dangling out the door.

"I just had the carpet replaced back here. I've had a certain fantasy about this van and a beautiful woman." Kai was looking at the sunset, but his hand was on my thigh, stroking up and down. I didn't know what his fantasy was, but if he kept touching me like that, I was thinking I'd like to find out.

"Mmm...what fantasy is that?"

He swung his gaze to me and I saw his eyes were looking a shade more green than hazel, a tell-tale sign he was turned on already. His hand slid up higher, almost underneath the hem of my shorts. "I want to make love to you in this van, with the roar of the waves right outside, the only light coming from the moon over the water." He cupped his hand over my jaw, threading his fingers into the hair at the nape of my neck. "Ready to be my fantasy come to life, Ono?"

My stomach dropped while my heart lodged in my throat. I wanted to give him his fantasy, but I also was nervous about being in public. An act so intimate seemed out of place here in a public parking lot. My indecision must have showed on my face.

"Hold that thought. Let's enjoy the sunset, do our meditation, and then decide. I think when you see how quiet it is out here, you'll see why I chose this spot." He brought me in for a kiss, his tongue doing a fine job of convincing me. He pulled back and settled further into the van, resting his back on the inside wall. He pulled me between his legs and brought my back to rest on his chest.

"Close your eyes and relax," he whispered in my ear. His hands moved my hair to one shoulder then traced down my arms, leaving goose bumps in their wake. Lips found my shoulder, kissing their way up my neck before nibbling on my ear. His hands massaged up my thighs, then my arms, never going under my clothing. With my eyes closed I was able to focus on his touch, enjoying the way he used his hands and forearms to rub down my skin. The long, sweeping strokes seemed to keep time with the waves crashing on the shore, audible from our man-made cave.

When his hands finished with my limbs, they curved up to cup my breasts, lifting them and pinching my nipples through my shirt and bra. My eyes flew open, thinking someone would see us. I was surprised to see that the sun was down, pitching the parking lot in complete darkness. No other cars were around us and not one person was walking on the paved path along the beach. The closest street light was half a mile down the lot.

"The beauty of the off-season, baby. I get fewer shifts, but there's no one on our beach at night." Kai was still playing with my breasts, but I knew he was holding off on going further until I made up my mind. I felt like I was sitting at the top of a rollercoaster in that moment before the ride pitches down into a stomach lurching drop. My heart was pounding and I wanted to do it. I don't know why I hesitated, other than a lifetime of conditioning that what we were about to do was irresponsible and possibly illegal if caught.

But the spirit of the Care Dares and Kai's 'you only live once' mentality was starting to rub off on me. How often in life would I get a hot lifeguard wanting to make me see the stars inside a vintage VW while we listened to the ocean crash in front of us? I wanted to live in the moment for once and forget about the future.

Before I could change my mind, I drew my hands to the waistband of my shorts and slid them down my legs, shimmying to get them completely off. The ocean breeze tickled along my skin, reminding me of my nakedness. I clenched my legs together, making sure I wasn't flashing anyone who might just happen to be out on the beach in the darkness. Kai's hands tightened on my breasts, knowing my answer was yes.

Then his hands left my breasts to strip my shirt up and off. The clasp of my bra was released and Kai slowly slid each strap off my shoulders and down my arms, whipping it off entirely.

I sat frozen, knowing I was completely naked in full sight of anyone who could see in through the side door of the van. Kai's arms came around and covered my breasts.

"I won't let anyone see you, I promise. I'll make this good for you," he whispered, a hitch in his voice.

I closed my eyes, hoping that would block out our public environment and let me relax. I could tell how much he wanted this and I wanted to give it to him. I decided to trust him and trust myself to enjoy this experience. Time to try new things.

All that courage fled when he used his feet to spread my legs apart and hold me spread eagle in front of the door. All I felt now was a rush of sensations as one hand left my breast to travel over my stomach and down between my legs. He continued to tweak my nipple while his other hand moved up and down my slit, spreading the wetness I didn't even know was there. I may have been apprehensive about this public display, but my body was all in.

Kai continued to trail his lips along my neck and shoulder, whispering encouragement to me in the form of dirty talk. I freaking loved it.

"You're so wet for me, Ono. I can't imagine how beautiful you'd look right now if someone were to walk by and see you spread for me."

I groaned out loud, turned on by his both his words and his hands playing my body like a human ukulele. The groan was followed by a gasp as one finger entered me, thumb brushing across my clit. His other hand left my breast and joined the party in the Netherlands. He spread me open, while his other hand continued to pump in and out.

"Touch your breasts for me, Hessa."

I didn't argue or waste time being embarrassed. I reached up and cupped my warm breasts, making sure to copy the pinching and squeezing he'd started. Between the two of us, I was close to the edge, ready to fall and not sure I could contain my moans. Hoping to keep the noises to a minimum to avoid attracting attention, I bit my lip.

"It's okay, no one is out there. Let go, baby," he whispered, the words nearly strangled in his throat.

He thrusted with two fingers, thumb keeping time on my clit for just a few more seconds before I exploded. I writhed on the floor of the van, hands abandoning my breasts to hold his magic hands to my center.

"Kai, oh God, yes..." I was groaning and talking, unaware of how loud or quiet I was. Frankly, I didn't care anymore. All that mattered were the waves of pleasure rushing through my body as his fingers kept up their rhythm.

And then Kai was laying me down, reaching over to slam the door shut. He opened the windows running along the top of the van, letting in the ocean breezes. I was too out of it to ponder what he was doing. Before I knew it, he'd ripped his shirt off and was pushing down his shorts in great haste. I wanted him to slow down so I could enjoy the show. His body was magnificent and I wanted to take my time perusing it.

"What's wrong?" I managed to ask. I feared that maybe someone had seen us, but then why would he be getting undressed? My brain was addled by the orgasm and nothing was making much sense.

Finally naked, he lay down between my legs, his forearms on either side of my head. "What's wrong? I just watched my woman enjoy the orgasm I gave her in my VW on the beach, no inhibitions left, spread eagle for anyone to see." He kissed me quick.

"Nothing's wrong, other than the fact that I need to be inside you before I blow."

I didn't even get a response formulated before he thrust into me in one powerful push. He groaned into my mouth as his tongue pushed its way in, intent on possessing me in all ways possible.

His fingers had felt wonderful only moments before but paled in comparison to the hard length pistoning in and out of my body, filling me completely. I wrapped my legs around his waist, my toes almost brushing the roof of the vehicle with each thrust.

Here in his favorite place, he seemed so much more alive, his face intense, his eyes lit up with a passion I hadn't seen before. I'd made fun of his barefoot habit prior to knowing him, but I could see that he just loved to be out of doors, like that was his natural state. If the strength of his thrusts were anything to go by, I was happy to take it outside any time he wanted.

Kai abruptly pulled out and sat back on his haunches. He pulled me upright and instructed me to sit on his lap. I slowly sank down onto his cock, locking my feet behind his back. He felt even bigger in this position and I loved it.

Sweat beaded on his brow, the heat in the van ratcheting up as we kept our bodies in motion, breathing the same air. He locked his gaze on mine, staring into my eyes silently, the act just as intimate as our lovemaking. In slow motion, he leaned his head down and sealed his lips to mine, his hips finally thrusting, impaling me fully on his shaft. Ribbons of pleasure wove through my body causing my legs to contract and pull me into him, helping to set a faster pace.

Moisture formed between our bodies, our skin slipping and sliding across each other. We were desperate for each other. Too involved in the moment to slow down or open another window. Kai's arms loosened around my back, sending me sliding down his thighs. I had a moment of panic at the loss of our rhythm. That is, until he rose up above me and laid me against the back of the driver's seat. He used his hand to guide himself back in, sighing as he slid home, as if he too, mourned the momentary loss.

I lifted my arms and placed them above my head, grabbing hold of the seat behind me to keep from slumping down the slick vinyl. His hands joined mine right before he slammed into me again and again, using the leverage of the seat to dominate me. I lost all track of time and setting, focused only on the coil of sensation at my core, desperate to break free.

"Come with me, Ku'uipo," Kai managed to grit out from above me. One hand left the seat and zeroed in on my clit, like he knew my body perfectly. Every muscle contracted and my body was strung tight right before an explosive orgasm rocked through my veins, shutting down all thought as I rode it out.

Moments later, I felt Kai slump down on top of me. My hands, now robbed of their strength, let go of the seat, causing our bodies to slide down to the carpet in a crumpled, sweaty heap. Neither of us seemed to care as we settled into each other, the frenzy from earlier simmering down to a low buzz of awareness and bliss.

After what could have been minutes or hours, Kai stirred, kissing his way across my stomach, each breast, and into the crook of my neck. I squealed, finally rising out of my sex-drunk stupor to giggle and playfully push him off.

Kai pulled me up and rubbed my neck, which had been lying at a funny angle jammed up against the seat back. I purred my thanks, taking stock of my limbs, coming back to the moment. Remembering where we were.

"Oh!" A hand shot up to my mouth. "How loud were we?" I whisper-yelled to Kai.

He took one look at my shocked face and burst out laughing.

"I realize my concern is a bit belated, but you don't need to laugh at me, Mr. Kāne." I was still naked as the day I was born, seated criss-cross applesauce in the back of a VW van after being thoroughly fucked by a hottie lifeguard in a public parking lot, but I could pull off righteous indignation any time. I put my hands on my hips and gave him 'the look'. The one all teachers had, either born with or developed over the years of dealing with unruly kids.

Unlike my students, the look didn't seem to have much effect. Or at least, not the one I was going for. Kai's eyes heated right before he leapt on me, tackling me back to the floor. His lips opened mine roughly and his tongue plunged in, commanding my acceptance. I didn't even think to put up a fight. I may play the role of a pearl-clutching rule follower, but one kiss, one look, one touch from Kai, and I was willing to toss my virtue aside for a shag or two in a parked car.

I guess I was finally living up to my nickname Hessa the Hussy. And the hussy I was just smiled wickedly as we went for round two.

Kai

The sex was beyond mind-blowing. I was speechless, completely flabbergasted that Hessa had allowed us to go that far in my VW at the beach. I honestly didn't think she'd go for it, and I was okay with that. I'd take Hessa any which way she'd have me. But after that display? I'd never be able to top that. Ever. Hell, I was never going to let anyone else in this vehicle again, lest they taint my memories here with her.

"How loud were we?" Hessa shouted. She was staring at me, her eyes wide, the fear evident. My eyes trailed down from her disheveled hair to her heaving breasts, then her beautiful pussy on display for me as she sat in my van.

Knowing I'd made her lose all track of where we were made

me feel puffed up with pride, happier than I'd been in a long time. I laughed, feeling light and blissed out, thoroughly amused by her concern.

When my laugh trailed off, I saw that her skin was flushed, showing red marks where my hands had marked her. A caveman sense of possessiveness came over me, intensifying when I saw the look on her face. I knew she meant to intimidate, like I was a naughty student, but all it did was turn me the fuck on. My cock perked up, sensing we weren't done here, not by a long shot. Ms. Woodland was about to be the one reprimanded.

As I attacked her mouth, I wondered briefly how she felt about spanking.

17

essa

The days and weeks flew by, highlighted by nights with Kai, my days dominated with the Care Dare program and talks of bringing it back. The newspaper article did exactly what Kai hoped it would. Concerned parents petitioned the school board to reinstate it and it looked like they would. We'd find out for sure when they met at the end of the calendar year to discuss the curriculum for next school year.

Seniors were starting their Care Dares and every single one was closely monitored by me and executed safely. I gave the information Bailey had found for me over to Jack, without explaining where I'd found it. He didn't like that much at all, but finally took the info saying he'd have to have his own guys find out who was behind the online dares through legal means if it was going to hold up in court.

Frankly, I was beginning to wonder if they'd ever arrest someone. The online dares seemed to stop and nothing else had happened. I was still planning to go through with my dare of singing in public though. I was determined to raise money for Gabe.

He'd come out of his medically induced coma and was recovering quite well. He was back at school, but seemed much more subdued after the accident. His mother had apologized to me when the newspaper article came out and it became apparent that neither I, nor the Care Dare program, was responsible for her son's hospital visit. She still had a huge bill however, and I was determined to help.

My sister came over quite a bit on the weekends and hung out with me like old times. I was already dropping the gut reaction of waiting for the other shoe to drop. She really did seem a changed woman, and for that, I was extremely grateful.

It was one Sunday afternoon, a week before my performance at Pacific City, when Rainna was lounging on my couch, entertaining Kai and I with stories of the crazy clients in her tattoo chair. I was sitting on Kai's lap in the recliner, savoring the feel of his hard body surrounding me. Our schedules didn't always aline well with his constantly changing shifts, but when we were together, we were seldom outside of touching distance from each other. If I'd been an outsider looking in, I would've been sickened by the sweetness of it all. As it was, I was addicted and falling for him. Hard.

"And then he just dropped trou and asked me to tattoo it on his dick! Can you believe that?" Rainna was gesturing wildly, totally engrossed in her story.

Kai winced, shifting below me, probably to hide his own appendage, frightened of a tattoo needle anywhere near it.

"Ewww...that's so gross!" I grimaced. "You didn't do it, did you?"

Rainna threw back her head and laughed. "No! Turns out, he doesn't like girls. I had to hand him off to Blaze for that one."

My jaw dropped. Blaze? If I remembered quickly, he was like six foot five and almost 300 pounds. "I don't get it."

Rainna started gesturing lewdly with her hands. "Well, to tattoo a dick, it has to be fully erect. I wasn't doing the trick, so Blaze...." She shrugged, trailing off and letting our imaginations complete the story.

I shuddered and Kai suppressed his mirth, his whole body shaking with the effort.

"Anyway, I have an idea for you two." Rainna clapped her hand, changing subjects so fast I was getting whiplash. My mind was still playing out the Blaze scenario like a train wreck you couldn't look away from.

"I'm not getting my dick tattooed. Sorry, Rainna," Kai deadpanned.

"No! Not your dick. That's for my sister's eyes only." Rainna winked at me. "I came across this kickass drawing of a ukulele. The wood grain of the instrument actually spells out Ku'uipo when you look closely at it." She paused for dramatic effect. "I thought you guys could get matching tattoos!"

She sat back, eyes glowing with excitement. She looked like she was going to explode, waiting to see our reaction.

I looked to Kai, who looked back at me. "I never really thought of getting a tattoo, to be perfectly honest."

"That's because you're perfect already, baby." Kai was looking at me with those hazel bedroom eyes. The ones I couldn't resist.

"Ahhh, that's funny coming from a freaking bronzed god." I nuzzled the side of his neck.

"Hello? Tattoo?" Rainna clapped her hands, startling me. "You guys are so gross. Pull it together would ya? I'm right here."

Without lifting my head from Kai's neck, I said, "You're whining dear sister. Weren't you just leaving?"

"Ugh!" She flounced out of the room. I kissed along Kai's neck, feeling his hand slide up my thigh and under my shorts. In the distance I heard Rainna yell, "I'll make appointments for you both next week!" Then my front door slammed, pulling me out of the sexual fog I was happily drowning in.

Kai stood up and carried me to my bedroom. "Don't worry, Ono, you don't need to get a tattoo, but I think I will. I want your name branded on me." He bounced me onto the bed and crawled up my body, pulling me back into the fog.

I was supposed to be putting the finishing touches on the songs I had to sing the following weekend, but in reality, I got very little done that afternoon.

During my last class of the day on Friday, I got a text from Jack asking me to call him as soon as I was able. The pit of my stomach clenched, wondering if another student had gotten targeted by the online daredevil who we thought had gone dormant. I was distracted the whole rest of class, forgetting to assign them homework over the weekend, to their delight. Before the last student cleared the doorway after the final bell rang, I had my phone out and was dialing Jack's office line.

"Jack Ramirez," he answered with a growl.

"Jack? It's Hessa Woodland." I tried to keep the warble out of my voice, but it snuck out, giving away my nervousness.

"Hessa. Thanks for calling me back." Jack's tone turned super friendly and I was able to take a deep breath. "We caught the guy!"

"Oh, thank God." I ran a hand through my hair, completely destroying my ponytail. "Did he say why?" I didn't care who it was, I just wanted to know why he'd endangered people's lives and targeted me in particular.

"Well, that's what I wanted to talk to you about. We've got him in an interrogation room right now and he says he'll only talk to you."

The sound of hundreds of high school students leaving school right outside my door faded away as his words echoed in my mind. Talk to <u>me</u>? What? Why?

"Hessa?" Jack's voice broke into my thoughts. "Listen, I know this probably sounds terrifying, but I'd be right there next to you in the room. A confession means this case would be a slam dunk. It would really help if you'd do this."

And that was exactly how I found myself sitting in a sterile interrogation room at the HB police station with Jack beside me and a disheveled young man sitting across the table, hands cuffed behind him. He was mid-twenties with dark hair that fell into his eyes every time he fidgeted. For the life of me, I couldn't place him. Couldn't figure out what any of this had to do with me.

Jack took the lead, just like he promised, pointing right in the guy's face. "So, I've got Ms. Woodland here. How about you quit wasting our time and tell us what happened?"

I'd never seen Jack with a criminal before and I never wanted to again. He was scary. Still hot, but totally scary.

The boy looked right at me and I could have sworn I saw sad, little boy eyes behind his obvious anger. "This is your fault!" he spat at me.

I jumped back, visibly shaken by his animosity toward me. "Wh-what do you mean?"

When he rolled his eyes, I knew I'd have to do better to get him to talk to me. I was the adult here. "Listen, I can see that you're very angry with me, but I don't even know who you are. I want to understand, so please explain it to me." I leaned forward, hoping he'd sense my sincerity.

He scoffed at me then leaned forward too. "You don't know who I am? That's hilarious. You ruined my life and you don't even know who I am?" He laughed, but the sound was dripping with rage.

Tears filled my eyes. I was no longer shaken by his behavior, just profoundly sad that he'd allowed his fury to rule his life. The kid clearly needed help.

His eyes widened when he saw tears welling up. "No. You do not get to cry. I'm the one who should be sad. You wanna know who I am? I was your student four years ago when you were learning the ropes of the Care Dare program. You let some sick fuck dare me to try out for the basketball team. He taunted me repeatedly, knowing I was too scared to actually go through with it. The whole team picked on me until I couldn't walk the halls at school without someone saying what a pussy I was for not even trying out!" He was out of control, spit flying out of his mouth as he shouted at me. "Your stupid little Care Dare program changed my life, and not for the better like you all tried to make it seem. I went to the school board and they said I had no case and they wouldn't shut the program down. I couldn't let you keep running it and hurting other kids."

He sat back, quite pleased with himself. He'd finally been able to release all the anger and shame he'd felt for four long years. And he'd done what he'd set out to do. The program was shut down and he'd shaken me to my core.

The tears spilled over and raced down my cheeks. I didn't bother to wipe them away. I figured I deserved them since I'd let this student down. If he was in my class four years ago, he must have been in my first class as the assistant to the prior English teacher that handled the program. That wasn't an excuse in any way, but it did open my eyes to the danger Kai had tried to warn me of. I wasn't sure how to make this right, but I knew he deserved an apology.

"I'm sorry. I'm sorry the dare backfired. I'm sorry you were bullied and I never saw it. I'm sorry for every part I played." I wiped the tears away and became the teacher he should have had four years ago. "But here's the truth. Being mistreated doesn't give you an excuse to hurt other people. You hurt innocent people and mistreated them, just like you were mistreated. Do you see the irony there? You're going to go to jail for it."

He grunted in disgust, looking away from me.

I slapped my hand on the table. His head whipped back. "You have an opportunity to do things right this time. Do your time and then do better. As long as I see you trying to be a better person, I will be around to help you. Do you understand what I'm saying?"

He paused, sizing me up.

"I'd take that generous offer, if I were you," Jack put his two cents in. "You won't get a better one."

The young man considered, then gave me a slight nod, accepting my offer. I nodded back, meaning every word I'd said. I'd visit while he served his time and I'd mentor him, help him get the skills he needed to cope with life in a more constructive way when he was out. I could only help as much as he'd let me, but help I would.

Jack and I left the room and went back to Jack's office. I slumped in the chair and Jack patted me on the shoulder. I guess that was the extent of consoling you could expect from a tough-guy cop.

"Go home to Kai, talk it out, and then let it go, Hessa. This was not your fault."

I sighed, feeling a weird mix of relief that the investigation was finally over, but also acutely sad that I'd played a part in this guy's twisted reality.

"Maybe it's a good thing the program's shut down after all." I hefted myself out of the chair, grabbed my bag and headed home to do just what Jack suggested.

Kai

I'd been working hard to keep Hessa from a full scale freak out over her fundraiser or the conclusion of her former student going to jail. We'd talked it through incessantly Friday night, along with all of the Beach Squad that I'd called in for reinforcements, and we'd finally gotten it through her head that it was unfortunate, but she bore no responsibility for his criminal actions. She could help him now if it made her feel better about 'failing' him as a teacher, but he had to shoulder the responsibility for everything else.

With that squared away in her mind, she turned her attention to the fundraiser for Gabe. The event had gotten a lot of press and we were expecting quite a turnout tonight at Pacific City. We'd gone through her playlist, making sure she had a few covers in there that everyone knew and could sing along with. She also planned to debut three songs that she'd written and composed herself. She was most nervous about those, but I'd heard her practice them and they were incredibly beautiful.

Her songs were very slow and sensual, which fit her voice perfectly. She had the kind of voice you could listen to over a glass of wine and candlelight. So pure and velvety.

I told her I'd meet her at the venue so she could get ready in peace and I could make sure all the equipment was set up how she wanted. When I got to the courtyard, I saw over a hundred white chairs set up facing a small curved stage. White twinkle lights were strung overhead which I thought would set the mood perfectly for her songs.

Fiona, the newspaper reporter, was supposed to be there as well to cover the fundraiser. I talked to my lifeguard buddy Dean the other day and he said Brinley had approached the professional DJ that worked the IVP volleyball circuit. She told him all about the fundraiser and Hessa's music. He said he'd stop by with some friends of his that were in the music business.

I didn't tell any of that to Hessa though. Her nerves were strung high enough without knowing reporters and music industry peeps would be there watching her. I'd been having to force-feed her all week. My girl loved food as much as I did, so I knew she was nervous when she turned down the dinner I made her the other night. I even tried to bribe her with ice cream. She only got down a bite for two before turning me down flat.

The thing is, I knew she'd shine. Hessa had this energy about her that everyone could feel. She was intelligent, funny, and so damn kind. She would bend over backwards to help someone in need. And on top of all that, she was an amazing artist. Her lyrics made you sit up and listen, connecting to the emotion that she poured into each verse.

There was no way she could fail tonight. She was that good.

Unless of course, she choked because of nerves.

Whatever it took, I would not allow that to happen. I'd stand up on the stage and make her look in my eyes the whole time she was singing. I'd pep talk her the whole time. I'd have her Squad form a protective circle around while she sang so she couldn't see the audience. Whatever. It. Took.

18

essa

I was going to puke.

I had on the prettiest outfit I'd ever had on, thanks to Bailey doing some shopping for me, and I was going to get vomit all over it. Figures.

My hair was already done in loose curls down my back, which was already a departure from my usual ponytail. But my hands were shaking so badly, I couldn't even get make-up on my pale face. I tried to do a black winged eyeliner which ended in an unfortunate poke in the eye. Then I tried to get eye drops in my eye to get rid of the redness, which just burned like crazy, making both eyes water. Tears streamed down my cheeks unchecked, leaving streaks in my foundation.

I'd have to put a paper bag over my head and cut out a hole to sing through. There was nothing for it.

The doorbell rang, making me jump. I ran as fast as I could to get the door. The tight, black, mermaid style dress didn't allow for a long gait, so it took twice as many steps to get there. I swung open the door and nearly fainted from relief when I saw Esa standing there with her big make-up case.

"Help me!" I cried, rather dramatically.

She took one look at my face and cringed. "I got here in the nick of time, I see."

I grabbed her arm and dragged her in. She set up in my bathroom, telling me to sit on the closed toilet seat and practice my meditation breathing. I tried, I really did, but between the spanx I had on and the fluttering of my heart, I was just happy I didn't pass out.

Esa swiped all kinds of goop across my face, using an endless supply of brushes and sponges. Then she started shoving pins in my hair, jabbing me in the scalp repeatedly. When she was all done, I sprang up and opened my eyes to take a peak in the mirror.

"Oh my God!" I didn't even recognize myself. I looked like a sultry 1930's era singer. My hair was pinned to one side, letting my curls cascade over one shoulder onto the ample cleavage showing, thanks to whatever push-up/platform/girdle thing Bailey gave me to wear. My make-up looked airbrushed on with bright red lips completing the look. The black dress I wore hugged my barely contained curves all the way down to my knees before it flared out in an asymmetrical hemline around my ankles.

Esa was smiling ear to ear like a proud mama behind me. "You look stunning, Hessa."

"I do. I really do," I answered in a hushed tone. I was in awe of what was looking back at me in the mirror. Maybe I could do this.

"Amazing what a little armor does for a woman's confidence, huh?" Esa winked at me, knowing I was scared out of my mind.

I twirled around to hug her, almost lifting her off the floor. "You are the very best. Thank you."

She laughed, hugging me back. "Happy to help. Now let's get your heels on and I'll drive you down to Pacific City."

When we arrived in the parking garage below the courtyard, it took three tries before I hefted myself out of Esa's low car. Between the dress, the stiletto heels, and the butterflies in my stomach I wasn't functioning properly.

"Did you bring the barf bags?" I threw over my shoulder to Esa after I'd successfully climbed out of the car.

She barked out a laugh, not realizing I was serious.

I'd decided in the car ride over here that I was going to go to my happy place. I was going to bury my head in the sand and pretend that this whole thing was happening to someone else. I wasn't sure how psychologically healthy that was, but I figured it might help me refrain from puking on my audience, and that right there was worth it. I'd get professional help later.

With that new mindset in place, I got my music sheets out of the trunk, grabbed my water bottle, and sashayed my glorious ass over to the escalator. Time to face the music. Literally.

The first person I saw when the escalator deposited me at the top, was Kai. He was standing right there waiting for me, dressed in a white linen button down shirt over black pants. In his hands was a huge red hibiscus flower.

"You look incredible, Ono. Good enough to eat." He leaned in close to whisper in my ear. "Which I will do tonight to celebrate." Then he placed the flower in my hair behind my ear. "My island girl."

The man knew just what to say to calm my nerves and make me feel like I could do no wrong. We hadn't said those three little words yet, but I felt the love. I could totally bungle this thing tonight and he'd still be totally into me. That was a beautiful feeling.

Hand-in-hand we walked over to the stage, exchanging hellos and head nods with the people already milling around.

"Quit counting people," Kai said out of the side of his mouth. My jaw dropped. How did he know I was doing that?

"Look here." Kai gestured to the first two rows of seats closest to the stage. They all had reserved signs on them. When I did a double take, Kai clued me in.

"Your girls reserved the seats for them and your sister. Figured if you got nervous, you could just look out at us and pretend the rest of the people weren't even here."

"That's so sweet, and so perfect. I'll have to thank them big time later." I was touched everyone was being so kind and thoughtful. They were thinking of things I hadn't even considered, knowing this was a big step for me. The heavy pressure on my chest eased up a bit, allowing me to breathe a little deeper.

I put my music sheets on the little table up on the stage, checked the microphone height, and talked to the AV guy about doing a sound check. I kept my back to the chairs, letting them fill up without watching it happen and panicking.

Eventually, Kai led me off to the side of the stage and put his hands on my face, careful not to mess up my hair or make-up, but demanding my full attention. My legs were shaking and I swallowed hard. I let all the terror I felt show through my eyes.

"I know, baby. I know you're scared. But I want you to take a moment, okay?" At my frightened nod, he continued. "Close your eyes. I want you to picture Gabe in that hospital bed. How frightened he and his mother must have been. Now picture Ms. Martinez' face when you hand her the check from tonight. See how her eyes light up and the weight is lifted off her shoulders? You did that, Hessa."

Kai gives me a slight shake and I can feel the energy shift. I can feel the scared being tamped down by the joy I'll have doing something that would mean so much to my student. Instead of my failure in the form of a student now in jail, I had the opportunity to do good, to set things right. His words strengthened my resolve and my spine straightened with renewed purpose.

"You are a beautiful, smart, courageous, strong woman. And your students get to see that tonight. Let us see you, Ono. Give us the gift of your music."

Then he leaned down and kissed me lightly. I kept my eyes closed a few moments longer to bottle up this empowered feeling, knowing I'd need it as the night went on. I didn't ever want to lose this feeling right here. That moment when you know you have to do something that scares you to your core, but once it's over, you know you'll never be the same. What was life without risk?

I finally blinked my eyes open, seeing Kai smiling at me like I was all he needed in this world. The white lights above cast a romantic light on a beautiful evening. Waves crashed nearby and the palm trees swayed in the gentle breeze. Perfection.

I gave Kai a saucy wink and headed to my stage.

As I reached up to grab the microphone, with the worst timing ever, my feet sent up a red flag warning. They were dying a thousand deaths in these damn heels and I suddenly understood Kai's dogged determination to remain barefoot no matter the dress code. Tonight, of all nights, was about getting out of my comfort zone so I figured I'd go whole hog. The heels went flying as I kicked them off, and the crowd whistled and hollered, probably wondering what this performance was gearing up to be.

I tilted the mic, placed my fingers on the keyboard, and looked up, putting all thoughts of wardrobe behind me. A sea of faces looked back at me, but all I focused on was Ms. Martinez in the first row, next to Esa and Ivan. I looked to the right and saw Kai seated next to my sister. The full Squad was here, along with a sea of lifeguards who were probably recruited by Kai.

"Welcome friends!" I hollered into the microphone. "I'm Hessa Woodland, an English teacher at Surf City High. We're all here to listen to some great music...let's hope." The crowd laughed right on cue. Self-deprecation was always a crowd pleaser. "We're also here to raise money to help support one of my students who was in an unfortunate accident. So focus your audio, don't be parsimonious, and you can Google what that all means later. Enjoy!"

I launched right into my first cover, making a few errors on the keys, but knowing most wouldn't even notice. And if they did, oh well. I was doing my best. I closed my eyes and melted into the music, losing myself to the words and the melody. I found myself more at home on the stage than I ever thought.

After three songs, I took my fingers off the keys and took a sip of water. Time to rip my heart open and let my guts spill out onto the floor.

"Up until a few months ago, no one, absolutely no one knew that I wrote songs in my spare time. It was a creative release for me. I loved stringing words together and putting them to music. So much of my writing had to be academic, but with songwriting, I could break all the rules. Sing about all the emotions. When I was dared to sing in public, I believe it was meant to be a way to humiliate me. But I won't be shamed about my music any longer. In fact, I wholeheartedly thank the misguided soul who dared me. It was the push I needed to do what I should have done a long time ago." I took a long cleansing breath. "So without further ado, I give you three of my own songs."

I played the opening bars on the keyboard to the first one when my fingers locked up and my heart seized. I couldn't do it. Singing other people's songs was one thing. Singing the songs I wrote from the heart, not thinking at the time that anyone would ever hear them? That was insanity.

I lifted my head and frantically searched out Kai in the crowd. I couldn't find him. His seat was empty.

Abandoned.

My heart dropped, a dead hunk of muscle of no use in my body without my music and my man.

I had one second of sheer terror and profound, crippling loss before the first strum of the ukulele hit my ears. I whipped my head around and saw Kai strolling onto the stage, playing the intro to my song. He had it memorized because I'd written it and gone over it endlessly while we sat on the beach and watched the waves a few weeks ago. It was a song about the ocean and the flow of life. The dichotomy of the frenzy of crashing waves and their calming rhythm to the observer.

My heart kickstarted and my fingers came back to life. I picked up the tune on my keyboard and joined him. His eyes never left my face, his warm smile grounding me and reminding me of what I was really doing here. This was about facing my fears and helping my students. My songs could suck and I'd still survive. But together, we'd finish what I'd started.

I launched into the lyrics, my voice stronger than before, my island boy playing a duet with me, the ocean our backdrop.

I wondered briefly how I got here. Whose life was this? How could so much change in so short a period of time?

Perhaps the answer was in my song: each crazy event of late felt like chaos while I was in it. Waves tumbled rocks, no rhyme or reason to the way they crashed. Sand shifted, shells scraped unsuspecting ankles, and riptides pulled people in. The water splashing, the relentless pounding, and the hiss of the foam dispersing. The ocean waves all perfectly described the chaos of my life at the moment. Yet through a different lens, each wave was just a soothing rhythm that calmed the mind and acted as a balm for the spirit.

So here I was.

Instead of sitting idly by, I was going to jump the waves, splash around, and enjoy the water.

ai

Hessa's performance was epic. Not only did she look and sound like a dream, but you could feel the audience getting into her songs. Her lyrics had a way of pulling you in and relaying a feeling. Some songs were introspective, others were about the great unifying emotion of love.

By the end of her three songs, the crowd jumped to their feet applauding. From my corner of the stage, I sat back and just watched her light up. It was like I could physically see her self-confidence jumping by leaps and bounds as the applause extended out. Her face was split in a radiant smile. She threw kisses to her Beach Squad girls in the first row. She bowed and then came over to me.

I felt like my chest would burst with how proud of her I was. I wasn't a brainiac English teacher, and therefore didn't have the words to express how I felt. So I gave her what I could: my love. I kissed her beautiful red lips, took her hand in mine, and walked her off stage.

I wanted to tell her I loved her, but bit my lip to keep the words from spilling out. This was not the time, nor the place. She deserved to be in the spotlight and I wasn't going to distract her from this moment.

The moment we got to the chairs, people swarmed around her, wanting to congratulate her and talk to her. I got pulled away in the rush and went back to the stage to pack her things up for her. If I couldn't be by her side, I'd be in the background supporting her.

As time went on, the crowd began to disperse. I made my way back to Hessa as Brinley and two men I'd never seen before approached her. The guy in a suit introduced himself as a Sony Music executive.

"I enjoyed your songs, Ms. Woodland. If you have more, I'd like to hear those too. Give me a call." He talked fast and handed her a business card with a number handwritten on the back.

Hessa stared down at the card and then back at Mr. Suit. "Th-thank you!" She quickly shook his hand and watched him walk away, jaw hanging open.

Before anyone could say anything, the Beach Squad girls rushed Hessa, grabbing her and jumping up and down. Squeals of excitement filled the air as I backed away. That huddle was no place for a man. The other guy that was with Brinley backed away just as quickly and came up to me to shake my hand.

"DJ Lush. That your girl?" His curly blond hair was in some sort of mohawk formation, probably quite flammable from all the product in it. I may not see the appeal for that type of hair, but he pulled the look off.

"Yep. Looks like things just broke for her." I couldn't seem to wipe the smile off my face. I watched her jumping and laughing with her girlfriends, the jubilation of facing her fears and coming out of it a massive success lighting her up from within.

"Make sure you tell her to get her music to that guy ASAP. He doesn't give out his number very often, so he must've really liked what he heard." With those parting words he moved to walk away.

I stopped him momentarily with a heartfelt thanks and fist bump. I knew he'd been the one to get him here tonight.

"Thank Brinley. She's one of a kind. Figured if she liked Hessa, she must be pretty special too."

I looked back at the huddle of girls, seeing them with new eyes. I always thought girl squads were just a gaggle of girls that laughed a lot and took ridiculous selfies. I should have known that Hessa wouldn't be involved in that sort of thing. The friends she surrounded herself with were the real deal. They supported each other and loved each other unconditionally. We'd all be so lucky to have friends like that.

And then Bailey screamed "Selfie time!" and they all crammed together while she extended her arm and snapped a picture on her phone.

Hessa

After the concert, I'd meant to celebrate with Kai back home, but I basically collapsed into bed in a sleep coma. All the nerves from the week leading up to the fundraiser, along with actually performing in front of a crowd, had sapped my energy.

When I woke up Sunday morning, Kai wasn't in bed next to me. I pouted, wanting to snuggle and enjoy a weekend where we didn't have to rush off to work. A noise outside my bedroom had me sitting up. In walked Kai with a tray of food and a single lily in a vase. A love-sick, goofy grin split my face.

"Good morning. Ready for breakfast, my superstar?" Kai sat

the tray on my lap and climbed carefully into bed with me. He picked up one of the cups of coffee on the tray and sipped, watching me intently.

"Morning. Thank you for breakfast in bed. Why such special treatment?" I surveyed the eggs and toast, cut up fruit, and coffee laid out before me.

"Figured we'd celebrate today, starting with breakfast. Plus, I gotta make sure you don't forget about little ol' ukulele-playing me when you meet some hot celebrity guitar player when you sell your first song." Kai winked at me and I knew he was kidding, but I hoped he didn't have any doubts about us.

I took a big bite of eggs and slurped my coffee. "I'd totally reassure you right now, but I've barely eaten all week and I'm starving!" I said with a mouthful of deliciousness.

Kai laughed and settled against the headboard with his coffee. I loved how easy it was to be around each other. I could be sleep disheveled, shoveling food in my mouth, and he still thought I was adorable. That made him a keeper.

I was still chewing my last bite when Kai hopped up and took the tray off my lap.

"Chop, chop. Time to get dressed." He reached down and pulled me out of bed despite my whining and feet dragging.

"What is with you, Kai? Where are we going in such a hurry?" I was normally a much nicer morning person, but after last night's craziness, I was hoping to have some downtime today.

"Just get dressed and I'll tell you on the way." He cupped my face in his hands. "Trust me, you'll like the surprise." Then he kissed me and I tried to deepen the kiss by running my tongue along the seam of his closed lips. He groaned but pulled away.

"Don't distract me, woman," he growled. Then he slapped me on the ass before leaving the bedroom.

Kai pulled the car up to the curb and I glanced around, not recognizing where we were in Costa Mesa.

"Are you going to tell me now?" I'd asked him repeatedly in the car, and each time he'd smirked and kept silent. The boy knew I liked to have things nice and orderly. I think he enjoyed stringing me along with no clue what was going on.

"Payback's a bitch, just so you know," I told him before grabbing my purse and exiting my own car.

The fucker just laughed. I rolled my eyes and pretended to be disinterested when he came around and wrapped me in his arms.

"Don't be mad, Ono," he whispered in my ear. "It's time to put your name on my body."

My head popped up, almost whacking him in the chin. "Tattoo?"

He smiled, grabbing my hand and tugging me along to the tattoo shop a few storefronts away that I hadn't seen yet.

"Oh my God! You're going to do it now?" I was running alongside him to keep up. I was so excited yet oddly nervous about this step in our relationship. I mean, come on. He was incorporating me into a tattoo that would forever be on his body!

When we reached the tattoo shop, he pushed me up against the building, his eyes burning into mine. I was so caught up in his warm body pressed against me, I didn't feel the cold bricks running along my back in the early morning air.

"When you love someone like I love you, Hessa, you don't wait to tell the world. And you aren't afraid to tattoo it permanently on your body."

My eyes widened and my heart started beating out of my chest. I wasn't sure if I'd heard him correctly. His eyes morphed into that green shade I'd come to love. His voice sounded like sweet music.

"I love you, Ku'uipo."

And then he kissed me, his hands holding my face, then traveling south to pull my hips into his. This felt like more than a passionate kiss from a lover. It was a sacred promise. A vow to always love me. To always back me up when I faltered. To keep me safe. To have someone jump in the waves with me.

I would have spent the day with him like that, canoodling on a public street, but my sister rudely interrupted with a lewd whistle from the shop doorway only feet away.

"Get a room, you two! Actually wait, scratch that. Get in here and get your tattoo first." She winked at me and then went back inside, giving us a moment to collect ourselves.

Kai was breathing hard as he pulled back, putting much needed space between us. I grabbed his shirt and pulled him back in, not ready to break the moment. Making sure I had his full attention, I told him clearly, "I love you too, Kai."

I could have sworn his eyes dilated and his face relaxed. It was like my words were the magic he needed hear to finally be settled.

"I will always miss my island home, but with you here, the mainland is now my home." He kissed me one last time and then dragged me into the shop, holding the door open for me, ever the gentleman.

Back at my house, I put on the lingerie I'd asked Bailey to pick out for me last week. The plan had been to put it on last night after my concert, but I figured tonight would be even better timing. He'd lit my soul on fire by saying he loved me. We'd gotten tattoos. Yes, even I got a tattoo. I'd called the Sony executive after our tattoo session with my sister and I had a meeting set up next week with him.

We had a lot to celebrate.

I pulled the red lacy thong up my thighs, loving the soft scrape it made on my skin. I couldn't wait for Kai to take it back off. A matching, red bustier pushed my breasts into the stratosphere. I was hoping it wouldn't cut off my air supply before Kai got to see me in it. On top of that naughtiness I pulled on my tightest black pencil skirt, the black high heels Kai had once commented on, and a white button down shirt.

As all busty girls know, usually a button down shirt is a definite no-no because of its peek-a-boo nature. But for tonight, that was part of my seduction plan. My black glasses firmly in place and my hair in a topknot completed my naughty schoolteacher look.

My first attempt at seducing Kai had ended in humiliation, but I was a smart girl and I learned quick. No alcohol beforehand this time.

I rushed around the room lighting all the white candles I'd bought last week. I'd bought out the store of their gardenia and jasmine scented candles. As a final measure, I synced my phone to my speaker, selecting a Hawaiian Spotify playlist. I was hoping to recreate a taste of his island home. One day, I hoped we'd go to Hawaii together and I'd get to experience his childhood love.

Kai was due home any minute from Ivan's house. He'd had to try on tuxes with Ivan and Dean. As badly as I wanted to see him in a tux, I was saving that reveal for Esa and Ivan's actual wedding day. Besides, I needed time to prepare my den of seduction, gosh darnit.

"Hessa?" I heard Kai drop his keys on the table by the front door.

Show time, baby.

I sauntered slowly out of my bedroom, meeting him in the middle of the living room.

"Wha--"

I placed a finger on his lips, shushing him. "You're late, Mr. Kāne. Looks like you're getting detention today."

His eyes widened and I swore I could see the wheels turning in his head. The green of his eyes came out and the air thickened around us, letting me know he'd figured out my game.

"Yes, ma'am," he conceded, doing a damn good impression of contrite student.

I grabbed his shirt and led him to my bedroom where I'd show him exactly what detention entailed in Ms. Woodland's private school. I kicked the door shut, not that anyone would be barging in, but it made the whole thing a bit more naughty behind closed doors. I looked over my shoulder at him and saw his eyes widen, taking in the candles, the music, the overall ambiance.

"Sit." I pointed to my bed, then crossed my arms over my chest, knowing the buttons were threatening to pop, giving him an eyeful of cleavage.

He sat on the edge of my bed, pausing to adjust the front of his shorts, for what I couldn't possibly guess.

I stalked over to stand directly in front of him, heels putting my breasts right in his face.

"Eyes up here, young man." I smirked, unable to hold back the curve of my lips. This was funny as hell, yet still hot, truth be told.

Kai dutifully brought his eyes up to meet mine. His held no amusement, only heat. He liked the sexy dominatrix teacher routine. Interesting.

"In detention, you have to do as I say, no matter what. Is that understood?" I tilted my head and gave him 'the look', one eyebrow up in question.

"Yes, ma'am. I'll do absolutely everything you tell me to. And nothing more." Now he was smirking at me, challenging me to keep up this charade in order to get what I wanted too.

I shrugged my shoulders, looking around the room before zeroing back in on Kai. "It's a bit hot in here, don't you think? Take my shirt off."

Kai's hands slowly trailed up my thighs, over my hips and between my breasts. Buttons popped open, one by one down my front. He took his time opening my shirt, finally revealing the red bustier by pulling the shirt down my arms.

His hands left my body to rest as clenched fists on his thighs. "Anything else, ma'am?" he gritted out between clenched teeth.

"Hmm...you know I've been pretty stressed this week with all these misbehaving students. I could really use a massage. Can you handle that?" I moved my breasts just a fraction of an inch closer to his face.

"Depends. Are you looking for me to use my hands or my lips?" He was focused on my ample cleavage, tantalizingly within reach.

"Mmm..." I let a groan slip out before I could pull it back. "How about both?"

"As you wish, ma'am." He spun me around and the way he manhandled me so easily made my stomach melt and my pulse race. I was only five minutes into this role-play and I already wanted to say forget it. I didn't want to be his strict teacher any longer. I wanted him to take control of my body and have his wicked way with me. My plans for becoming a dominatrix went up in smoke.

His hands were tracing down my spine, unhooking the bustier and releasing my breasts. I could finally breathe with the restriction gone. That only lasted for one inhale because Kai took that opportunity to start his massage. Of my breasts.

He knew just how to pay the right amount of attention to get me writhing on his lap. I reached down and shimmied my skirt up to bunch around my waist, no easy task given the tight nature of the fabric and the girth my thighs spread to when seated. With only my sheer thong covering my assets, I felt every nerve ending attune to what was going on in Kai's pants. I ground down harder, finding enough friction to take me right over the edge if he would just continue the breast massage a bit longer.

Of course, he chose that moment to stop, his hands lying demurely on the top of my thighs. "What else can I do for you, Ms. Woodland?"

I had to restart my brain several times to remember what

game we were playing and the appropriate response. "I think there's only one thing left for you to do." I stood up, backed up a few paces away from him, and pushed my skirt down to the floor and stepped out. "It's time to fuck me, Mr. Kāne."

Kai

She stood there, in just her red thong, black heels, and glasses. Her face was flushed and her breasts were pink from my hands. I wanted nothing more than to throw her down on this bed, sink into her warmth, and fuck her senseless. I'd never had a sexual fetish before, but now that I'd had a real, live sexy teacher standing before me in the flesh, and nothing but the flesh, I realized that I could quite get into this roleplaying thing.

"What? No spankings in detention?" I asked innocently.

Her eyes grew big, the thought of spanking obviously never entering her mind, which I loved about her. So kinky and yet so innocent at the same time. I stood up, pulling my t-shirt over my head and tossing it to the floor. My zipper was the only sound in the room as I slowly removed my shorts. I palmed my erection, loving how her eyes dropped down to watch, entranced.

I stayed where I was, letting her watch as I stroked up and down my length. "Take off your panties." I was done taking orders. Done playing her student.

She pulled her eyes away from me and stepped out of her thong. She bent down to take her heels off, but I stopped her, barking out another order. "Keep the heels on."

She straightened up and let me look at her. Just a few short weeks ago, she'd been so shy about showing me her gorgeous body, trying to cover up and hide from me. I was happy she'd gained confidence in herself and realized I idolized every curve she had.

"Get on the bed and lay down on your back." I stepped to the side to allow her access to the side of the bed. She climbed onto the bed on all fours, ripping a groan from my chest at the sight. When she flipped over to lie on her back, she had a proud smirk on her face.

The smirk died a quick death when I startled her by lifting her legs and placing her heels on my shoulders, pulling her to the edge of the bed. We both groaned at the intimate feel of each other. No clothes, no barriers, just skin on skin.

My hands danced along her legs, feeling her from ankle to hip before settling on her waist in a tight grip.

"I love you, Ku'uipo." Then I thrust into her, giving us both the pleasure we'd been waiting for. I set a rough pace, not able to hold back any longer. Her breasts bounced with each thrust, which made me take her harder, just to see the show.

Hessa reached up and ripped her glasses off her face. She was groaning in between each slide of my cock into her body. One of these days I was going to make her sing to me while I made love to her, just so I could hear that beautiful voice wrap around me. I fully intended to introduce spanking to our bedroom fun, too, but tonight, I didn't want or need any of those things.

I just wanted her.

I wanted her orgasm. I wanted her fancy words. I wanted her eye rolls when I went anywhere barefoot. I wanted to watch her eat and moan with pleasure. I wanted to help her grade papers on the weekends. I wanted to watch her bend over backwards to help her students. I wanted to take care of her and worship her for as long as she'd let me.

When I couldn't hold back any longer, I dropped my hand between her legs and gave her what she needed. Her legs tensed on my shoulders and her eyes went soft. "I love you too, Kai." And then I saw the pleasure sweep her under, her back arching, offering me a view I'd never get tired of.

"Always..always...always..." she muttered incoherently.

I tumbled after her, knowing she was mine forever, just like the new tattoo on my back stated.

The End

(But not really because the Beach Squad grows in Book #4, Beach Babe Billionaire AND the novella Handcuffed Hussy!!!)

ABOUT THE AUTHOR

Thank you so much for reading Barefoot Chaos! If you loved it, please support the series by leaving a review on Amazon or Goodreads so other readers can find it and enjoy it too. Reviews help other readers determine if a series is to their liking and they help indie authors sell more books so we can keep writing. If you hated it, please disregard this entire paragraph. :)

If you'd like to know more about me or the other novels that I'm writing, please come stalk find me on Facebook or join my reader group on Facebook called Marika Ray's of Sunshine for all the best stuff first. You can also find me in-person, on the beach in Southern California, scoping out the hottie lifeguards. For research purposes only, I assure you.

If you want to take your stalking to the next level, here are other places you can find Marika:

Newsletter - http://bit.ly/MarikaRayNews

Amazon - https://www.amazon.com/author/marikaray

Goodreads -
https://www.goodreads.com/author/show/16856659.Marika_Ray

Bookbub - https://www.bookbub.com/authors/marika-ray

Instagram - https://www.instagram.com/authormarikaray

ALSO BY MARIKA RAY

Beach Squad Series:

1) Sweet Dreams

2) Love on the Defense

3) Barefoot Chaos

* Novella-Handcuffed Hussy

4) Beach Babe Billionaire

5) Brighter Than the Boss

* Novella - Christmas Eve Do-Over

Steamy RomComs:

Happy New You

The Missing Ingredient - Reality of Love #1

Mom-Com - Reality of Love #2

Desperately Seeking Househusbands - Reality of Love #3

Small Town Steamy RomComs:

Love Bank - Jobs From Hell #1

Uber Bossy - Jobs From Hell #2

Sweet Romances:

The Marriage Sham

The Widower's Girlfriend-Faking It #1

Home Run Fiancé - Faking It #2

Guarding the Princess - Faking It #3

Lines We Cross - Nickel Bay Brothers #1

HANDCUFFED HUSSY PREVIEW

(BAILEY & JACK)

Beach Squad Series Novella

Jack

In my world as a cop, things were either black or white. Right or wrong. Then Bailey arrived, challenging all my principals. She had a mouth on her, the level of sass matching the exaggerated swing of her hips. I couldn't get her out of my head, even knowing she wasn't right for me. I tried to stay away, I really did. But once I had a taste, I kept coming back for more. Something didn't add up though and I was going to figure it out, even if it ultimately meant we couldn't be together.

Bailey

The only thing sexier than his dimple was the set of hand-cuffs the hottie detective threatened to use on me. If only he'd give me a chance to show him I was more than the tough-girl exterior I'd carefully crafted over the years. Oh yeah, and if I wasn't engaged in criminal activity that would land me in hand-cuffs...and not in sexy way. More like an orange jumpsuit way, and I can tell you now, no way in hell would I be caught dead in an ugly jumpsuit.

No matter which way this thing ends, I'll be in handcuffs. The question is, will Jack join me in the grey area? Or will I have to do the impossible and admit I was wrong?

CHAPTER ONE

Past - Bailey

The resident asshole was staring at me the moment he walked through the door of the science lab. I could tell he was the school asshole by the perma-sneer on his face and the way he walked into the room with an exaggerated swagger that only the coolest of cool kids adopted by the time they hit middle school. His was a well-practiced swagger by now, causing all lesser-than students to dart out of his way while flashing hesitant smiles, hoping for validation in the form of a cool-guy head nod in return.

I rolled my eyes and yawned, having seen this exact scenario too many times before to be impressed. Besides, I was pissed off, having been forced to attend a new school as a freshman, facing day one with less enthusiasm than my mom when she had her first mammogram. If I looked like I cared about this dipshit, I'd break from my pissed off routine and I was committed, goddammit.

I examined my nails, seeing the first chip in my black polish. I'd only painted them last night, you'd think I'd be chip-free for at least one day. Perfect. Messed up manicures fueled my pissed-off attitude. It was this thorough nail examination that made me miss the prolonged look from dipshit, right before he changed directions and sat down next to me.

It was the obnoxious mouth breathing that snagged my attention. I couldn't stand loud breathing and especially chewing. Ugh, it was so disgusting. Like nails on a fucking chalkboard.

I looked up to find him leaning over his small desk to enter my air space, smirk a bit more pronounced as he looked me up and down.

"You're new."

That's right, ladies and gentlemen, he led with the lamest line ever. It was so bad I would have laughed, but figured that might encourage his kind.

"You're observant, Neanderthal." I didn't bother looking at him since that's what he wanted me to do.

He chuckled hesitantly, probably trying to figure out what Neanderthal meant. Or maybe he thought I was just so overcome by his majesty's attention I couldn't squeak out more than three words.

"You got a name, beautiful?"

"I do. But you can't have it." The conversation continued, him talking to the side of my face, me talking straight ahead to the chalkboard.

"You like to play games, huh? I can think of a few games we could play," he drawled, then burst into obnoxious laughter.

I finally turned to him, drew as close as I could stand without vomiting, and made sure he got a nice view of my cleavage. I laid my first and last flirty smile on him. "How about we play my game first? It's called Go Fuck Yourself with Your Tiny Dick."

He jumped back like I'd physically attacked him, brain trying to process rejection. His leer turned to a sneer. "Like I'd have anything to do with you, freak." He jumped up and stomped across the room to another chair, whispering to his friends and looking back at me.

I just smiled and winked at his buddies, excited to be making friends already.

Another warm body slid into the chair next to me, this time a blonde girl. Not a mouth breather. She had a very peaceful way about her, sitting in her chair observing the goings-on of the room.

When she glanced my way, I asked, "You got something to say to me too?" Might as well weed her out right now. Her preppy, good-girl outfit didn't bode well for a blossoming friendship with the likes of me.

"Yeah, I do. I love your outfit!" She leaned forward, a mischievous gleam entering her eye. "Teach me how to do that."

I tilted my head. "Do what?"

"How to tell those assholes to go 'eff themselves! I've been wanting to do that for years, but I can't seem to get the words out."

I squinted, wondering if I wanted to go there. If she was worth breaking my pissed-off streak. Something about the way she held no judgement as she looked at me pulled me in. Made me want to open up to her. Made me want to give this new school, this new life, a solid try. What did I have to lose?

"All right. Here we go. Let's do this." I smiled the first genuine smile in years, pleasantly surprised my face remembered how to do it.

I think I was ten when it dawned on me for the first time that I was a real-life, living cliché. My mom was a poor, single mother, raising me the best she could with two jobs and all the stress of keeping a home and raising a daughter without any help. My dad had escaped the cliché life when I was just a baby, choosing wide open pastures instead of diapers and sleepless nights. I never knew him long enough to miss him, but his absence left a raging pit of resentment toward him and all his kind.

The anger and lack of parental supervision led me down a rough path. My friend circle was full of the "unsavories", mad at the world and making sure everyone knew it. I fit right in with my teased out Afro and my brightly colored clothes. The more ripped up and mismatched the better. And that was only middle school.

My mom finally stepped in the summer before my freshman year and called my bluff on the escalating bad behavior. She moved us out of state, all the way to California where she got a better job. I had to enroll in a new school without any familiar faces.

Adding insult to injury, she also forced me to start going to church with her, saying she'd failed me by not taking me before then. I rolled my eyes, crossed my arms and sent out dirty looks and negative energy, gaining me few friends. I actively fought it, I really did, but after only a few weeks a particular family took my mom & I under their wing, my mom all smiles and gushing profuse thanks. I went kicking and screaming but went I did.

And the only reason I put up with such coddling was because it was Esa's family. After our friendship pact that first day in science lab, we were inseparable. My mother rejoiced, having barely saved me from being a pregnant high school drop-out, or some other such malady she swore I was destined for. I mean, I saw her point, but a little optimism from my own mother would have been nice.

Esa's mom and dad, Mr. and Mrs. Grant, treated me like their own daughter, telling me I could be at their house anytime I wanted, no prior invitation or even knocking on the door required. Since we lived only a few blocks from each other, they might have gotten more than they bargained for when I was at their house pretty much every day. When they started regularly stocking my favorite brand of yogurt, I knew I'd found my second family.

They were a churchy couple, praying at the dinner table, attending church every week, and volunteering their time at the homeless shelter. They always dragged Esa and I with them, which we agreed to since they were so nice all the time. The least we could do was volunteer alongside them. I wasn't down for the church stuff as I didn't believe in it, but I took to the volunteering like cotton and spandex.

It was at the homeless shelter that I gained insight into a life I vehemently did not want to experience. The hard shell I'd carefully constructed around my heart crumbled when I saw the conditions in which these people lived. I had perfected the tough-girl schtick around my peers, but the truth of the matter was that I was a marshmallow underneath that façade. Only Esa, her parents, and the people at the homeless shelter ever saw that side of me.

By the time I graduated high school, I'd lost my angry undertones thanks to Esa's parents and the volunteering, but I'd kept my signature sassiness. I'd also kept my love of flashy clothing and funky sense of style. I was accepted into the fashion design program at UC San Diego, where I'd room with Esa in the freshman dorms.

Life was the best I'd ever known those first two years of college. I was living with my best friend, attending a gorgeous university, and pursuing a career I loved and would keep me off the streets.

All that came to a screeching halt when Esa texted me one morning.

Esa: *Rady Hall ASAP. I need you.*

This was enough to cause my heart to race and a heavy sense of doom to take residence in my stomach. I acted tough, but Esa was the rock in this relationship. She didn't need me for anything, except for comic relief, perhaps. If she said ASAP and that she needed me? The world was ending.

I grabbed my backpack and ran out of my lecture hall right in the middle of a riveting discussion on verb usage. I was willing to ruin perfectly good high heel boots just to get to Esa in the shortest amount of time possible. My cardio training was seriously lacking on the best of days, so I thanked the Gods Rady Hall was only a few buildings away.

I whipped open the double doors, Wonder Woman style, and charged in to find Esa and two police officers in the main hallway. Esa was slumped against the wall, her hand covering her mouth. I didn't see any handcuffs, so I figured this was good news.

"Esa? What happened?" I reached her side and pulled her into a hug. She wouldn't look at me, so I looked to the police officers for an explanation. They looked at her first and she nodded her head.

Looking in my direction again, with somber expressions on their faces, they changed my world in a single sentence. "I'm sorry to tell you, Mr. & Mrs. Grant died in a car crash this morning."

Everything around me dimmed. The officers continued to talk, but there was no sound coming out of their mouths.

I blinked.

My heart beat once, then twice.

On the third beat everything came rushing back, the sounds around me drowning out my thoughts that made no sense anyway. Doors opened and closed in the long hallway, the officers were speaking over each other, and my labored breathing was echoing in my ears.

Then I felt Esa shudder in my arms and it was like a lightning bolt to my brain. She was sobbing, her face buried in my chest, her body curled up like she was protecting herself from attack.

I didn't have time to fall apart or to grieve. This wasn't about poor little charity case Bailey any longer. I needed to be Esa's rock now. So I took my first steps into adulthood by shaking off my shock, my grief, and my renewed anger. For now, I'd welcome in the numbness. I asked the police officers what had happened. I asked what we should do next. I got their business cards. I made a list in my head of who I needed to call. Family, friends, our professors for extensions on assignments and tests, the mortuary, the cemetery, the lawyers, the bank. The list was endless.

And all the while, I held Esa, whispering over and over that everything would be all right. The Grants had taught me how to love without limits and to sacrifice for others. In their honor, I'd continue to do that, starting with Esa.

3 Years Later - Bailey

Shattering glass woke me up from a delicious dream about a pool boy and his long stick. I rolled out of bed and glanced over to see the clock read three a.m. I threw on a robe out of habit before rushing out of my room. Now that Esa's boyfriend Ivan lived there in the house with us, I was used to covering up outside of my room.

I raced down the stairs and came up to Esa, huddled around a corner, peering into the front living room area. I peeked over her head and saw Ivan huddled in the middle of the shattered glass from the front window.

"It just says 'Bitch'," he growled. I assume he meant the red brick he held in his hand. He picked his way across the glass to us, then moved us into the kitchen where Esa called the detective she'd been working with.

She'd had a break-in at her hot chocolate shop, her car vandalized, and now this. Someone wasn't too happy with her.

Which was crazy. Esa was the nicest, most level-headed person I'd ever met. She was the peacekeeper in our group of friends, always looking to include everyone and make sure everyone was happy.

Hell, if anyone should have a stalker it should be me! I just said things like I saw them. Said what I felt and thought about the repercussions of my actions later. Flirting was second-nature. Esa affectionately called me 'sassy' or 'feisty'. The word most people would use was less kind.

The doorbell rang, and I went to get it, leaving Ivan in the kitchen comforting Esa. I'd always loved my short, red and black silk robe, but I'd never been happier to be wearing the sexy thing than when I opened the door to Mr. Tall and Handsome.

The man standing before me had to be the detective working with Esa. She'd told me earlier that he was cute, but damn, she'd massively undersold it. He had jet black hair, brown piercing eyes, and the kind of lips you wanted to taste over and over again. His lips threw me. He held his lean, muscular body in such a rigid posture, alpha male attitude coming off him in waves. And then there were those sensuous lips that just didn't match.

One dark eyebrow raised, clueing me in that I'd left him standing there, the silence stretching out.

"If you're here to rob Esa, please hit me up instead." I turned on the charm, the flirt I always had at the ready. I extended my hand, pulling him in the door and dangerously close to me when he took hold of it, expecting a handshake.

"While I appreciate the offer," he drawled, glancing appreciatively at the open collar of my robe, "I'm on the other side of the law. I'd use handcuffs, doll."

He winked, then marched off to the kitchen to find Esa.

I blinked a couple times, trying to come to terms with that much sexiness at three o'clock in the damn morning. He was clearly a match in the flirting department, and I was intrigued.

Very intrigued.

Naturally, I followed his fine ass, highlighted in worn denim. He spoke to Esa and Ivan, then moved around the front living room collecting evidence. I wouldn't say I was watching him like a total creeper, but I was highly observant in wanting to make sure he didn't make any mistakes. My close supervision was for Esa's benefit entirely.

He was efficient with his movements, sure and confident in everything he did. I was certain my flirting had caught his attention, but it wasn't enough to deter him from the job at hand.

Considering the state of the butterflies in my stomach and the sexual desire pinging through my veins, I was impressed with his focus.

And irritated. What's a girl gotta do to get his attention?

When he was done, he told Ivan that Esa needed to have someone with her at all times. Between Ivan and I, we'd make sure that happened. As a side bonus, maybe being around Esa even more than I already was would put me in close proximity to my new detective crush.

As Jack was leaving, I muttered a bit too loudly, "How do I get myself a stalker? I'm thinkin' I'd like some police protection too." Esa and Ivan cracked up laughing. Jack pretended he didn't hear me, but when he reached the front door, he looked over his shoulder at me and lifted one side of his luscious mouth in the hot-guy version of a smirk.

Oh, he'd heard me all right. There was no mistaking the fire in those brown eyes.

He shut the door, instantly making my heart drop at the loss of potent eye candy. I cheered myself up by realizing I'd scored in this first round of the Flirting War. This thing with Jack was just beginning.

Download Handcuffed Hussy now!